MARRIED BY WIND

ARRANGED MARRIAGES OF THE FAE

ANGELA J. FORD

Cover design by Franziska Stern

Wrapped hardcover illustration by Ireen Chau

Married by Wind

Go back, daughter of sand.
Avoid the curse.
Return to your land.

I

THE GOD OF WIND

White sand stretched like a path pointing to the river, which sparkled under the pinkish hue of sunrise. Rays of golden light graced the spiked cacti, rugged bushes, and stunted trees, warning the nocturnal creatures that it was time to return to their burrows. Sunrise was my favorite time of day, not only because of the riot of colors that swept across the sky, but also because it was when I saw her.

She sat cross-legged on a multicolored rug, the light glowing on her brown skin. Her white scarf had fallen off her shoulders, leaving her arms bare. Pots of dyed ink sat in a neat row in front of her while she held up a strip of white wood and painted the colors of the sky.

In other lands, I'd seen artists paint with brushes on smooth paper, and in comparison, they'd view her work as rudimentary. It wasn't her skill I admired, but her actions. The way she wrinkled her nose when concentrating, using her fingers to blend each color until they mirrored the sky. Her brow furrowed while she worked, and she had a habit of staring up at the sky, contemplating, as though she saw something I didn't. Impossible, for I was the god of wind, and she was a mortal. A mortal who drew my attention.

I blew over her painting, making it dry, and teased her silky black hair out of its braid. Tucking loose strands behind her ear, she laughed. "You're relentless today."

She always spoke to me, which buoyed my ego, especially since mortals didn't know I existed. I wanted to reveal myself to her, but it was better to stay invisible and watch.

I swirled in a circle, and she sat up straighter, then shielded her eyes as she stared across the desert. The look in her deep-brown eyes was wistful, speaking of desire and unfulfilled dreams. I could not look at her for long without the finger of guilt poking my mind, so I returned my attention to her painting.

Beneath her fingers, a new shape took form. My heart swelled with pride as she painted the silvery mountain where I dwelled, what the mortals called Fae Mountain. They weren't wrong. I'd come from the halls of Val Ether, where the fae lived, sent to bring wind to the desert. The gods had warned me against my detrimental fascination for mortals, and they'd be furious if they discovered what I'd done.

"Ulika!" a voice hailed from the direction of the river.

The hungry joy of creativity evaporated. With a sigh, Ulika gathered her pots of paint while I sent her skirts dancing around her legs. An ache swelled in my chest, that old, familiar hollow of loneliness and longing. It wasn't natural to be jealous of mortals and all they had, but she made me want more.

To dispel my souring mood, I hurled myself toward the river. White tents and clay homes dotted the shore, for most of the desert tribes lived near water, but not all of them. I slowed to waft my winds over an old man floating on a raft, waiting for fish or death, who knew.

"Thank you, wind," he croaked, waving a suntanned hand.

At least he expressed some gratitude. Not all did. Some cursed my winds when they blew hot, as was often the case in the desert of Iscaria.

On the curve of the bank, curly-headed boys floated tiny clay boats with sails made of cloth. I blew over them, sending the boys shrieking and splashing into the water, clamoring to see which boat would win. For half a moment, I toyed with sinking them but, with a chuckle, left them alone.

I rushed through the camp, overturning pots, spreading the ash of campfires, and tangling loose hair, chortling as a series of shouts followed in my wake.

In one of the larger tents, shadows kissed, then intertwined. I paused, my mood for mischief vanishing. I was a powerful god with the ability to blow my winds across the desert and send myself to any location in the world I wished. Yet I was alone.

The mortals had companionship, children, and love. They had short and hard lives, focused on survival, searching for purpose and improving their lives for the next generation. I had freedom and eternal life, yet I clenched my teeth. A burning sensation heated the back of my throat. A god should not be jealous of mortals. My envy smoldered into anger, and no longer in the mood for pranks, I hurled myself away from the riverside, deep into the desert.

By the time my anger cooled, the sun had fully risen in a blaze of glory, and I was lost, which was exactly what I wanted. One trick of the desert was that the sand was ever shifting, and even though I whirled across it countless times, there was always something new to find. This place I did not recognize, nor the crack that ran along the desert floor, widening as I followed it.

The roll of thunder boomed, jerking my gaze to the azure sky. It was crisp and clear without a cloud in sight, but the rumble of thunder came again. Stones clattered and sand shifted as I came upon a cluster of boulders, piled up like a sacrificial altar.

Curious. The stones presented a temptation, challenging me to knock them over. Gathering my winds into a vortex, I swirled in a tight-knit circle until I slammed into the rocks. They exploded with a low boom and then scattered, revealing a gaping hole.

Interesting. Hovering above the hole, I waited, pulling back in disgust as a foul odor leaked out. A heavy voice bellowed from the deep, and then with a shriek, something emerged. It blasted into me like a storm, its winds swirling with mine. I tried to fly out of reach, but the menace whirled me around with it.

As I struggled to free myself, I came face-to-face with a horned darkness with red eyes. I'd never seen such a creature before, and a sudden fear turned my struggles to panic. With a roar, it hurled me across the desert, and my world went black.

2
ULIKA

Fae Mountain loomed like a monster in the pale streaks of dawn, jaws wide open to swallow me whole. Jagged rocks hung down like teeth, drops of dew dripping like saliva. Tugging on the reins, I pulled my camel, Nika, to a halt and slid off her back. A pointed rock jutted out of the sandy soil, and I tied Nika to it. She had a tendency to roam, and I did not want to be alone. At least, knowing the mute animal waited for me outside the mountain was a comfort.

A faint breeze stirred the still air, and tiny fragments of sand brushed across my bare toes. Shaking the dust out of my sandals, I adjusted my scarf before approaching the entrance. The breeze grew stronger, gusting with an eerie howl as it echoed through the bowels of the mountain. Goose bumps broke out across my skin, and my neck itched. It was just my nerves, my confidence waning now that I'd arrived at the forbidden place.

Legends claimed the fae had asked the spirits to create the mountain as a barrier between the desert and the Frost Mountains. Any who wished to cross from the land of heat and sun to the summits of ice and snow were cursed unless the spirits blessed them to proceed. I guessed the tale was born because of the unending feud between fae and mage, for rumors of wild magic were impossible to tame.

My intent wasn't to cross into the land of the fae, but for the truth. Other tales told of a sacrifice that would please the spirits and allow them to grant a boon, and I desperately needed a favor. No one could help my tribe except for an immortal spirit, and I'd come to offer a sacrifice—myself, if needed—in exchange for their salvation.

Soon I'd know whether my journey across the sand dunes was a waste of time or an answer to prayer. Hope awaited within the mountain, and I clung tight to faith as I stepped out of the blistering sun into the cool shade.

A path sloped up as crevices let in a halo of filtered daylight. The roar of the wind increased, a high-pitched wailing that made me want to turn around and flee. I clasped my fingers together to keep them from shaking, even though the wind whipped through my skirts, leaving my teeth chattering from the chill.

I was a daughter of sand, used to the heat of the sun on my face, warming my dark-brown skin. Heat, not cold, was my lifeblood. I shivered as I moved higher, rubbing my hands over my bare arms, wishing I'd worn something warmer. But the cold was only a minor discomfort if the legends were true. I tried to focus on what I'd gain if I succeeded, but flashes of death and destruction haunted my memory.

My parents were treasure hunters, and Mama believed that once, a rich civilization had dwelled in the desert until something destroyed them and scattered their wealth. I disagreed, choosing to believe the spirits had sprinkled treasure in the sands to give us blessings to discover. My younger sister, Anat, agreed with Mama, and now, after what had happened, I did too.

My tribe had built a city of clay on the banks of a lush oasis. But now we had nothing.

I closed my eyes against the memory of buildings crumbling, the screams of those crushed to death, and the wails of the survivors who had lost so much. The wind in the mountain echoed the sound like a mockery of grief.

I set my jaw and continued, putting one foot in front of the other as the air thinned, and then came the whispers.

Go back, daughter of sand. Avoid the curse. Return to your land.

The gusts grew stronger, pulling at my ebony hair, tugging at my dress. The gentle path turned uneven, sharp rocks poking up, determined to make me go back. My breath came short and fast as I avoided the traps and a cold sweat dripped down my back.

My skirt caught on the edge of a rock, and I fell, the cloth tearing with a loud ripping sound. My cry of surprise turned to pain as my palms and knees scraped across the stone. Hot flares shot down my arms and legs, and a smattering of rubble poured over the drop-off. A sob swelled in my throat, giving way to anger. Wiping my blood-smeared palms on my torn skirt, I stood, checking to ensure the treasure I'd tied around my neck was still secure.

It was.

Guilt racked me as I continued my journey, tentatively eyeing the drop-off on one side. The cave within the mountain was growing darker, and the item I'd stolen hung heavy around my neck. I hoped it would be a worthy gift to appease the spirit that haunted the mountain.

Suddenly, the path ended at the edge of a cliff, and the shadowy light faded even more. A boulder loomed above me, and I leaned against it, puzzled by the sudden end of the path. Perhaps this was far enough and it was time. The howling had stopped; the whispers faded. It was now or...

Something winked just above me.

I craned back my head, catching the faint glow of something warm and rosy. The path didn't end; no, it only led up to a ledge. Using my sense of touch, I searched for a handhold for my fingers. Sure enough, I found a crevice and a foothold for my feet.

The air was still, as though the spirit that watched me had grown tired of my determination. Best to ascend now before it drove me away. As I climbed, that sense that I wasn't alone grew stronger. I was sure a presence watched, not malevolent but curious. Hopefully curious enough to reward me for my efforts.

When I reached the top of the ledge, I rolled onto my side, gasping for breath. A domed cave rose above me, and I lay on a circular ledge. Runes swirled across it, making up a design of vines that curled and twisted, foliage that appeared oddly familiar. On the far wall, where a shaft of light peeked in, a bush grew, covered in green leaves with bloodred flowers lifting their faces to the light. Its rosy glow had caught my eye when I was down below.

Even though the rest of the ground was rock, the plant had thrived. Impossible. The rock was inhospitable to anything but the toughest plants, and yet there it was, beautiful and strong, growing where it shouldn't. The sight of those flowers made a bittersweet memory bloom, but I quickly pushed down the emotions I didn't want to feel.

A spark of hope gave me a wave of strength, and I pushed to my feet. Moving to the middle of the ledge, I knelt and ran my fingers over the runes. Fumbling with the treasure around my neck, I freed the object from the sack and placed it on the ground. Slowly I chanted, words tumbling over my lips as I struck a match.

Flame hovered over my lamp, blooming bright as I begged the spirit to grant me a boon. Wind roared in the distance, steadily growing louder until it surrounded me and my ears popped. I shouted the chant as wind yanked at my hair and clothes, screaming like a demented creature. There was something frantic and fearsome about the voice, and my lamp burned brighter, stronger, the flame never wavering as though it was immune to the wind. Then suddenly, with a clap of thunder, the light went out. The wind stopped. And I was alone in the dark.

3
VINN

It was pitch-black inside the lamp. At least, I had a hunch that was what had happened. When she had lit the flame, a sucking sensation had come over me, and for the second time in a few months, my power was inadequate. First the wind monster that came out of the hole in the ground, and now her. Ulika. It was ironic that she was the woman I watched each morning at sunrise. Except I hadn't seen her for a while. Ever since the wind monster had bested me, I'd gone to my mountain to sulk and hide.

I still recalled its winds trapping me, whirling me into unconsciousness. When I'd woken, I'd been alone, and even though I'd flown over the desert again and again, it had evaded me. Something evil had come into my home, and I wasn't the only one who'd suffered. The tribes had also reaped the consequences of my actions, and now Ulika had come to my mountain to ask for help. Half-heartedly, I tried to drive her away. Even though her determination was admirable, I could not help her.

She'd used fire to draw me into the lamp, some kind of foul magic I couldn't resist. Odd, because she didn't have magic, yet she'd trapped me. Or perhaps I was the one who was losing my magic. The very thought made my heart sick.

Still, it was selfless of Ulika to come to my home, for her tribe called it the forbidden mountain and no mortal had dared cross the threshold. Her prayer was touching, but her actions would lead to repercussions I could not shield her from unless I drove her away. First, I had to persuade her to free me and second, make her leave. I could not entertain any other thoughts, especially because of what had happened before. The gods would be furious if they discovered I'd meddled in the way of mortals, except this time, it wasn't entirely my fault.

I stretched. The small space was tight and dark, and worst of all, it was difficult to draw breath, as though the darkness was choking the life out of me. Would she let me out? Did she know I was here? Mortals weren't supposed to know gods like me existed, but she did. How? I'd been careful, hadn't spoken a word, but perhaps her presence meant something. I let out a long breath, hoping she'd see my winds curl out of the lamp. My heart thumped hard as the world tipped and the blackness became less dense.

4

ULIKA

Clasping my hands together, I waited. The darkness was absolute and unnatural, confirming the legend of the mountain was true. A presence dwelled there, and it had heard my plea. Now it listened, pondering my request, and slowly the light returned in hues of gray until I made out the shape of the golden lamp. A twitch of guilt made me flinch, but I pushed it away.

Weeks ago, I'd discovered the lamp under a pile of rocks, and something about it had made me quickly tuck it into my bag instead of sharing the old relic with my parents. It was an oil lamp, shaped like the ones my tribe made, but gold instead of clay. I'd washed and polished it carefully, admiring the sloping curves and the slight weight to it. Originally, I'd contemplated using it to barter for better paints and actual brushes, but considering what had happened to my tribe, offering it as a sacrifice was the right choice.

A tendril of black smoke curled from the lamp. My skin crawled as I waited, but nothing else happened. The silence stretched, the shaft of sunlight returned, and my fears threatened to overwhelm me. I tried to keep still, but the bruises on my legs and arms stung as the adrenaline of my journey ebbed away. A prickle began behind my eyes. It was over. The spirit hadn't seen fit to answer my question.

With a sigh, I held the lamp up to the light. The gift was insignificant, and dust marred one side of it. I blew over it, then wiped it clean with my fingers.

The lamp shuddered.

I dropped it on its side as smoke curled out of the tiny opening. At first the steady stream was small, but soon it grew bigger and blacker, swelling into a cloud that blinded me. Coughing, I stumbled to my feet and waved my arms, feeling for the smooth wall. A need to run seized me, but just as suddenly as the cloud had come, it faded, replaced with a man.

He stood beside the lamp, wearing loose linen trousers. Tousled black hair hung almost to his shoulders and curled around his pointed ears. The shadow of a beard crossed his heart-shaped face, while almond-shaped eyes glared at me with a coldness that made me shiver. His fists curled, making the muscles on his arms bulge, and the hardness of his chest tapered down to his low-slung trousers.

I sank to my knees as I gawked at the man who was, oh gods, so familiar. What was he doing here, in Fae Mountain? And had he just come out of the lamp? My chest squeezed, and even though my breath was shallow with the pain of a broken heart.

I blinked back tears as memories swam through my mind: the rich scent of his skin, fragrant with spices; the way his lips curved up when he teased me; the warmth of his hand against my cheek; and his soulful eyes, brimming with knowledge as though he could read the secrets of my heart and would grant every wish.

His name was Vinn, and he was a traveler, a nomad, come to visit the tribe before he continued his journey. He'd enchanted us with stories, played music with the bard, danced around the fires at night, and taken a special interest in me.

During his brief visit, the friendship that bloomed between us deepened into what I hoped was love. He brought me desert flowers with hues of pink and yellow and red, showed me how to crush them and use their ink to paint. He rolled up his trousers and caught fish in the river and, unafraid to get wet and dirty, played in the mud with the children. The herbs and spices he shared were rare. My tribe had never seen them before, even when we'd traded with other tribes.

When he dwelled with us, the flavors of food and the colors of the sunrise were bright and vivid. Life and energy surged when he was near and even my parents admired him. Wanderer though he was, I waited, breathless, for him to ask them for my hand in marriage.

Then, one morning, he was gone. Without saying goodbye. There one day, the next, vanished as though he'd flown away on the wings of the wind. We all missed him, and Anat teased me about being grumpy for weeks. I did not know how to put into words what his leaving had done to me. Like a blade slicing my chest and leaving a deep scar that would not heal. Each morning, I waited and watched, but he never came back.

Even when Uncle Noah had returned from trading, he'd said none had seen or heard of a traveler named Vinn.

Now the light shifted over his corded muscles, and I should have looked away, but warmth suffused my face. He was handsomer than I recalled, with a presence about him that made him appear larger than life. As though he was more than just a man. My lips trembled as I fought to keep everything within me from shattering, but all I choked out was, "Why are you here?"

"Ulika." He sighed my name like a prayer. "Why are *you* here?"

He didn't sound remorseful, rather resigned, and anger punctured my next words. Anger because he'd left without saying goodbye. He didn't sound happy to see me or care that I was in love with him. "I came because of a legend, a story regarding the god of wind. I came to ask for help, and you appeared."

He cocked his head, studying me, and then his dark eyes narrowed ever so slightly, not with anger but sorrow. “I am the god of the wind, and this is my home.”

Frozen, I gawked at him while his words sank in. Was it a joke? But why would he appear in this place to tell me falsehoods? Alarm raced through me as I tried to comprehend his words. But the more I stared at him, the more my memories made sense of his claim. None of the other tribes had heard of him. He’d known stories that even Jadda, the oldest member of my tribe, didn’t know, and had brought plants and spices that did not grow in the desert.

If he was the wind, then he hadn’t left at all. He watched over me each morning, ruffled my hair, and dried my paintings as though he was trying to be near me. Then there was the faint aroma of roses and spices in the mountain. It smelled just like him, and he’d brought me some of the red flowers that bloomed on the bush. That was why the rosy glow was so familiar. My heart pounded as I became aware of the truth, but I needed him to confirm it. “How? You walked among us like a mortal.”

"Yes, well, all gods can take the form of a mortal and walk among them."

I squeezed my hands together, struggling to keep my composure even though my entire body shook. He'd given me his attention, then changed his mind and fled. For months, I'd ached for his return. "Why my tribe?"

Why me?

He must have understood my unsaid question, for he crossed his arms over his bare chest. "I never meant to hurt you, Ulika. Every day, hope shimmered in your eyes and I had to rip myself away before it was too late."

"You're the god of wind. You said you were a wanderer. You said..."

"I can't lie." He cut me off harshly. "I told you the truth. While the mountain is my home, I go where I please in the desert. I'm immortal, blessed with magic and power and everlasting life. Eventually, your people would ask too many questions, and the truth would come out. I don't age. I don't change. I am who I am. And you've done something to me with that lamp."

The awareness of him hurt so much it was hard to breathe. “Me?” I gasped.

He gestured impatiently at the lamp, then bent to pick it up, eyes narrowed as he studied it. “Yes, you.”

“It’s a lamp, a gift of gold,” I stammered. “A gift in exchange for your goodwill.”

His frown deepened.

I went on, forcing myself to forget about love and our prior relationship. What was important was the task at hand, and if he truly was the god of wind, surely he’d help my people. “I’m here because sand devils attacked my tribe, not once, but five times. The first time, they destroyed our homes; the second time, they drove away most of our livestock. We have nothing, and they keep coming back. My people are afraid to rebuild lest they return. We seek shelter in the caves to hide from the violent winds, and no one will help us. The other tribes have shunned us, claiming we bring bad luck and the sand devils have marked us. That’s why I’m here, to ask the god of wind for help, and apparently that’s you.”

His dark gaze left the lamp and lingered on my hair, which had come loose and tumbled down my shoulders. He scrutinized the scarf around my neck, and my torn dress, which showed off the cuts and scratches on my skin. I finger combed my tangled hair, self-conscious about my appearance. If I'd known he was the god of wind, I would have tried not to look so dirty and disheveled.

Vinn's expression remained unreadable as he asked, "What are you proposing? That I take this lamp and guard your people from the sand devils?"

I nodded. "You know my people; you've lived among us, even though it was brief. Please, help us."

Vinn glanced at the lamp as he considered my request. "I've seen these sand devils you speak of," he said at last. "But the cycle of nature must go on unhindered. If this enemy falls, a new one will rise in its wake. If I interfere, the consequences will be felt for generations."

"Please," I begged. "We will die."

"Death comes to all mortals at one time or another, Ulika," he said gently.

I drew a sharp breath, for my name on his lips would be my undoing. Words failed me as he advanced, and I backed away, but he did not stop until my back pressed against the rough edges of the wall, the rosebush only a few feet away. Panting, I inhaled, and his scent filled my nostrils. Vivid flashes of landscape and scenery burst through my mind, roses, blood, dark red, a tantalizing musk with undercurrents of citrus. My heart pounded so loudly I was sure he could hear it.

Vinn, the god of wind, towered over me, leaving just enough space between us to breathe. He held up the lamp again, a deadly caution in his tone. "Do you know what this is?"

I licked my lips, suddenly hot despite the chill of the mountain. My answer would change everything and nothing at all. "It's a lamp, a golden lamp."

Tucking it into his trousers, he threaded his fingers into my hair. Those familiar dark eyes roved over my face, studying me as though he could read my mind. Under his touch, his power, I wondered if I had truly known him at all.

He was close. Too close. Allowing me to see the flecks of amber in his deep eyes, the flare of his nostrils, and the curve of his wide lips. His knuckles brushed my cheeks, my lips, causing a surge of fevered desire to rush over me. Flashes of memory returned, of a time when I had waited for his kiss, the kiss that had never come. Blood roared in my ears as my pulse throbbed, as though I was standing on the edge of a cliff and if I let myself fall, there would be no going back.

Instead of kissing me, he let go and stepped back.

I gasped in a deep breath of disappointment, blinking to hide the tears that stung my eyes.

"You truly don't know what you've done," he relented. "I know you, Ulika. You're mortal, without magic, yet somehow you've performed it."

I waited, unable to speak even if I wanted to. He was focused on the lamp, not on our past relationship, which was how it should be. Then why did it hurt so much?

His shoulders slumped as he held the lamp between us, his deep voice softening. "Long ago, the lamp was hidden beneath this world, where no one would find it and put it to use. You found it and came here, and although I guess it was not your intent, between your words and the flame of fire, you've trapped me with this."

He trailed a finger down the curves of the lamp, slowly, tantalizingly, and I squirmed. Trapped?

"This is no gift," he continued. "It's a curse, and even if I wanted to, I can't help until you free me."

I gaped, my jaw moving up and down. Just my luck. The gift was a curse instead of a blessing. Panic swirled around me, and tears burned my eyes. I held them back by sheer will. "How do I free you?"

A breeze howled in the hollow above the bush of red flowers. Petals trembled, and some tore free, tossing and turning in the updraft as Vinn moved closer. He slid his arms around my waist, pulling me into an intimate embrace. I'd tried to forget about him and move on with my life, but when he wrapped his arms around me, all I could think of was how much I yearned for a future that included him. Warm fingers brushed my skin, and more flashes of lush scenery captured my vision. When he spoke next, his lips were next to the shell of my ear. "We must go to the gates of Val Ether and ask the gods for advice. Hold tight."

5
VINN

Ulika fit perfectly in the cradle of my arms, as I'd known she would. It was not the first time I'd held her like this, and being so near her again made me ache for what I could not have. Her head lay against my bare chest, and her silky hair was the only shield between us. Instead of shying away, she kept her arms fastened tightly around my neck. Even though it was likely she was afraid of flying, I preferred to think she enjoyed being close to me.

Wistful thinking made me recall the couple kissing in the tent, and the acts of love between mortals. It had taken all my willpower to hold back from claiming her lips with mine. Her anger burned like a smoldering fire, and I held back for I'd created a rift between us. It was no use reminiscing the past, because a future together was not possible. The fact that she'd returned to me to ask for help was a cruel twist of fate. Like a knife driven into my ribs and turned from side to side. I'd left because I didn't want to see the disappointment in her eyes and because I'd reached a turning point. I couldn't be with her without professing to her what she meant to me.

Love was a connection that went much deeper than physical actions. It was emotional and spiritual and physical. It was the kind of companionship and connection I'd never have because as a powerful god, I was meant to be alone and above the desires of mortals.

The gods would not be pleased if I brought a mortal into their halls, but I hadn't lied to Ulika. I truly did not know how to dissolve the bond between us. She'd trapped me with the lamp, causing an odd tie, as though an invisible string bound me to it, or perhaps to her. When she'd lit the flame, it had sucked me into the lamp. In the future, I'd have to be more careful around fire.

Her request was admirable, but it also worried me. If Ulika had known I set the sand devils free, she never would have ventured to my home to ask for help. It was a problem I'd considered for a time, since it was my responsibility to make them go away again. But how? They'd bested my winds, blown me almost into oblivion. I was a strong god, but I wasn't all-powerful. I was only the wind and evidently able to be captured by flame. Taking Ulika to the hall of the gods was an excuse to ask for their wisdom and advice. Soon all this would be over. The desert would be mine again, and I'd think twice before knocking over piles of stones that kept monsters from the void where they belonged.

Snowcapped mountains loomed in the distance, and the tang of the air turned sharp and crisp. It had been a long time since I'd visited the Frost Mountains, and usually I did around summer when the land was lush with new life. The gods would not be thrilled to see me. I hoped, on account of Ulika, they would be lenient.

6
ULIKA

Unsure what to do with my arms, I faltered before wrapping them around his neck. Despite my misgivings about being pressed against Vinn, my body craved his touch. As the wind grew stronger, I tightened my grip. A vortex whirled around us, reminding me of the sand devils roaring as they advanced, the sand stinging my skin from the violence they created.

Fear made my sweat cool on my back, and suddenly my feet left the ground. I squinted. Even though we were moving, a wall of whiteness surrounded us. I fought my panic and squeezed my eyes shut despite the urge to cry out and take back what I'd done.

When the idea of going to Fae Mountain had sprung into my mind, I'd imagined myself a hero. Despite the warnings, I'd woo the spirit with treasure and save my people. Instead, the gift I'd brought was a curse.

I'd never heard of Val Ether, and if Vinn was telling the truth, it was not the home of the gods my tribe prayed to. I'd done something impulsive in going to the mountain, but this time, it wasn't something small, like hiding the lamp. It was my fault, and I wanted someone to help me, to save me. Perhaps the gods would be fair, but if they were anything like the spirits, they gave nothing for free. They'd want something in return, and I had nothing to give.

Presently the air shifted, and I became painfully aware of Vinn's arms around me, how my body curved into his, the heat coming off his bare chest, and the way he smelled, rich and tantalizing. Warm. That was the word that came to mind as my feet touched solid ground again. He was warm, and I was cold. A chill wind blew like the breath of an ice monster. Still, I let go of Vinn as I opened my eyes, my jaw dropping at the scenery.

We were high up on a mountain where snowcapped ranges appeared in the distance and a crystal bridge sparkled over a ravine. Far off I thought I glimpsed an ice palace, glittering against the mountainside, but with the rays of sunlight, I couldn't be sure. Rubbing my hands over the thin material of my dress, I faced Vinn. "Where are we?"

He pointed behind me, making me turn around, and the breath left my body. I pinched the skin on my arm hard. This was all some dream, a terrible nightmare, and any moment, I'd wake up. Please wake up, I begged myself. Icy wind stung my suntanned cheeks and the lush grass beneath my sandaled feet was unlike the mossy tuffs that grew alongside the riverbank. Here there was no sand but green lands as far as the eye could see, only broken by trees or rock or snow.

Vinn strode toward the gaping mouth of the mountainside, which was less like the opening to a cave and more like gates. He approached the entrance, while I gawked at the statues, towering fifteen feet high, with faces like cats and horns on their heads like those of a ram. My legs went weak. This was too much. I just wanted to go home, where the scorching sun ruled over the desert and I'd find solace with my sister, Anat, sitting on the banks, gathering clay to make pots.

When Vinn reached the entrance, he must have realized he was alone, for he turned. “Come.” His words boomed like thunder, compelling me to join him.

Somehow, I moved to his side. He took my hand, to ensure he didn’t lose me, I guessed, and we stepped over the threshold together. A sudden sense of smallness came over me as I stared up, up, up at the mountain, stretching out in unending rock before me. It was nothing like his home, and even though no wind tried to chase me away, an overpowering sense of presence hovered, making me want to run. I was certain they had judged me and I’d failed the test. I was not worthy to walk within the halls of the gods.

Wide slabs of gray stone led down in a series of steps, and I hesitated, feet dragging as Vinn pulled me along. I wanted to tell him I’d changed my mind and beg him not to let me go down there. But the words stuck in my throat, which was as dry as dust. When I looked behind me, the statues had shifted. Instead of standing guard, they’d extended their weapons over the entrance, blocking us inside.

I had no choice and squeezed Vinn's hand. He glanced back at me, curls springing over his forehead. "You're afraid," he remarked. "It is natural to have fear when you enter the hall of the gods."

No sooner had he finished speaking, the thud of hooves resounded, and a creature, half man, half goat, walked toward us. He held a two-sided ax in his hands. Shaggy fur covered his hooves, horns sprung from his head, and a short tail flicked back and forth. He stood seven feet tall, and dark eyes glared at us. My stomach sank with dread, and I backed up, recalling, at the last moment, that the statues had shut the way out.

"You are not welcome here, Vinn," the half man, half goat growled, lifting his weapon in warning.

I pressed a hand over my mouth to keep the scream inside while Vinn stepped forward. "Step aside. I've come to speak to the gods of the mountain. You cannot bar me."

"You were banished long ago," the half man, half goat spat, taking a threatening step forward. "You are not one of the fae of this mountain. Begone, trickster."

The tension in the air thickened, hot and heavy like a midsummer day. I tugged at Vinn's hand, my lips too numb to form words. Shadows shifted, and suddenly a woman appeared. "Tallen, stand down. I'll take care of this disruption."

With a frown, the half man, half goat—Tallen—retreated, but I noticed he hovered on the edges of the shadows, where he could barely be seen.

The woman strode toward us, dark hair piled on top of her head, a long gown sweeping the floor as she walked. She was tall, stately, old, and carried a sense of presence with her. She briefly glanced at me. "Vinn. Why have you come? And why have you brought a mortal with you?"

Vinn didn't respond with words. Instead, he held up the lamp and placed it at the woman's feet.

An audible gasp came, not from the woman, but from voices that lingered in the shadows. Again, an eerie sense crawled up my spine. There were invisible others watching the conversation, noting what happened here.

The woman's eyes flashed, and she stared at the lamp for a long moment. When her sharp gaze met mine, I sensed my past, present and future were no longer private under her scrutiny.

"You trapped him with this?"

I licked my lips twice before responding. "It was a mistake," I protested. My voice lost and small in the expanse. "It was supposed to be a gift."

Her sharp gaze returned to Vinn. "A word, in private."

He let go of me and self-doubt clouded my thoughts: I shouldn't be here. But they didn't go far, just out of earshot, where a tiny pool of light graced them with a halo. They spoke in low whispers, hands moving urgently, and I sensed they were arguing. Whoever the woman was, she was like him, immortal, powerful. And Tallen had called Vinn a trickster.

7
VINN

It was a relief that Justice hadn't flat out turned me away, but I'd known showing her the lamp would gain her attention. We moved just out of earshot of Ulika, but even with her quiet voice, Justice's words cut like a sword. "What have you done?"

It was useless to pretend to be innocent, so I quickly summarized the freeing of the sand devils and how Ulika had come to my home and trapped me with the lamp. I left out the part about spending time with her and her tribe before, pretending to be mortal. "I need you to free me from the power of the lamp and tell me how to combat the sand devils."

Justice did not respond with scorn or pity, only spoke matter-of-factly. "What do you know of the lamp?"

"It's a curse. As I told you, she trapped me with her magic."

"You claim she is mortal, and you studied her but could not detect any magic?"

An inkling of discomfort made my heart beat faster. Had I made a mistake in bringing Ulika here and allowing the gods to judge her? Surely they meant her no harm. "No, even she cannot hide her skills from a god."

"I will be the judge of that, but this lamp is dangerous. It contains dark magic. You should have driven her away or summoned us the moment the lamp came into her possession."

I racked my mind, but I'd never seen Ulika with treasure. Plus, it was painful to haunt her every step, and I hated doing so when she did not know I was merely a breath away. "It all happened so quickly. She climbed the mountain and lit the flame before I could stop her. I thought she'd simply come to pray, and I don't know when she found the lamp."

"Excuses do not become you," Justice rebuked, her tone cold. "If you did not feel the shift in magic, it was because you were not paying attention. You are a god with great power, but the lamp has its own magic, and you must meet its demands before it lets you go free."

I frowned. "You speak as though the lamp is alive."

"In a way, it is. There are rules of magic that even I cannot break, but I will bend them to your advantage."

A weight left my chest. She was going to free me.

"There's more. You mentioned the sand devils. You are the god of wind. We sent you to the desert to watch over it, and you let an abomination into the world that endangers the mortals. It is only fair that you remedy what you have done and find a clever way to get rid of them. You'll find that if you'd been paying attention, you would have realized that the finding of the lamp and the coming of the sand devils are likely connected. Because of your actions, you and the mortal are bound together— she in finding the lamp and telling no one, you for setting the sand devils free. Both of you are to blame for this."

A sudden protectiveness rose within me. It had been impulsive to bring Ulika here, wrong to ask the gods for help. I set my jaw. "What plan do you have? Because it sounds like you're about to punish us."

She did not smile. "Come, let me examine the mortal and tell you together."

"Do not harm her," I warned, all the while knowing the measure of Justice's magic put mine to shame. She would do what she wished in her home, and whatever power I summoned would be futile against her.

"As if you care," Justice said mirthlessly.

I crossed my arms, a sudden anger rising, because I did care. But if the gods discovered I'd fallen in love with Ulika, they would use that knowledge against me.

8
ULIKA

At last their conversation ceased, and the woman faced me. "Come," she beckoned.

It was a command, not a request, and I straightened, closing the distance between us.

Up close, the woman stood a head taller than me, stately, like the statues, with thick hair flowing around her shoulders. It caught the hints of light that entered the mountain, yet the exact color was ever shifting. Her eyes were deep pools that left me with the sense she was much older and wiser than her appearance and yet the secrets she kept were locked deep within the well of her mind. Like Vinn, she had a presence about her, and I assumed she was a goddess. She held out both hands and took mine in hers, pressing them together.

Her hands, like the air in the mountain, were cold, and a shiver went up my spine, not from the cold but from her touch. I had the uncanny sense some kind of transference was taking place.

When the goddess spoke again, she addressed Vinn. "She speaks the truth. She has no magic. It was a mistake."

"And you will undo it," Vinn said carefully.

"I will not undo what has been done. It would take great power to break this curse, but why ask the gods when you can break it yourself? Vinn, she made a wish. You must fulfill it, and then you'll be free."

Vinn's jaw twitched. "I can't use my magic. It is limited."

The goddess held up three fingers. "You may use your magic three times, and then it shall be gone until the curse is broken. Furthermore, this is a lesson. Vinn, you are the god of wind; you go where you please, you blow where you wish, and you have no regard for anyone but yourself. You shall be bound to the mortal for the next three months so you can get a taste of what it is like to be them. It will help you consider the consequences of your actions before you are impulsive again."

I gasped. She didn't know that Vinn had already had a taste of what it meant to be mortal. I yanked my hands out of the goddess's grasp, my tone sharp. "What do you mean?"

The goddess held up the lamp, examining it from each angle as though it was a rare jewel. "You shall be bound for three months, or until you meet the terms of the curse."

Suddenly, it was hard to breathe. Spots danced before my eyes as her words sank in. Bound to Vinn for three months, to the man I dreamed of, who'd left without a word. Oh, how the gods played a joke on me. Was my life so amusing to them? I didn't know if I could stand being so close to him only for everything to end. Again. "How will I know we have met the terms?"

The goddess raised three fingers. "When the sand devils are gone, the lamp will dissolve the bond. Vinn, your magic will return, and you, mortal, will be free to return to your life."

"I beg of you," Vinn said, his voice low and rough, "bend the rules and dissolve this foul magic once and for all. Let us go our separate ways. I will still find a clever way to get rid of the sand devils, but don't force us to be together."

The goddess shook her head firmly. "The fact that a mortal entered your mountain and trapped you with the lamp means that something is wrong with you. You've become careless."

Threads of confusion and fear and sadness twisted my thoughts. Vinn didn't want this either. He'd left me for a reason, and this curse would be the end of everything. Clasping my hands together, I tried to reason with the goddess. "You have the power to dissolve the bond? Please, I only wanted to help my tribe and save them from the sand devils."

"And you, mortal girl, should have known better than to ask the god of wind for help. All magic comes with a cost, and this is the price you must pay."

I closed my mouth, stunned at her words, but her icy glare was focused on Vinn. She lifted her hands, and the air shifted.

The spirits of the mountain appeared. At least, that was who I assumed they were. They ranged in size, some part beast, part human, others with pointed ears, sharp teeth, horns, and hooves. My legs went boneless, and I sank to my knees, unable to look away from them.

"The spirits agree with me," the goddess announced. "Get out of my sight, lest I change my mind and have you bound in human form for life."

Without waiting for a response, she strode away, and the crowd of spirits slowly disappeared, one by one.

When I caught my breath again, I struggled to my feet. Behind me, the statues no longer blocked the gates. We were seemingly alone in the mountain and free to go. With trepidation, I faced Vinn, and my heart sank. He stared into the gray shadows of the hall, clenching and unclenching his fists. When at last he'd regained self-control, he said, "Come, it's time to return."

9
VINN

Ulika slumped in my arms as I whirled us back to my mountain, and it wasn't until we arrived that I realized she was unconscious. I wanted to hold her until she awoke but, sensing the inappropriateness of that, instead laid her down gently in the circle of runes. No surprise, the hall of the gods was too much for a mortal to handle, that and their unexpected decision.

Scowling, I studied my rosebush, the one treasure I'd taken from the Frost Mountains. The color and beauty and scent of it reminded me of days of old, when I was younger, without an assignment, and frolicked in the gardens with the fae. I grew up among them, and they treated me as one of their own. Even my magic was not unusual, for there were many who had their own: ice, stone, fire, and even ink magic. The rosebush reminded me that sometimes one must endure thorns to reach the loveliest flowers, but in the end, their beauty is worth the bloodshed.

I tried to remind myself of that lesson as I paced, waiting for Ulika to wake up. Part of me wanted to apologize to her for how the gods had treated us. The wiser part of me tossed it away. Gods did not apologize. I'd done nothing wrong, but the gods of Val Ether had embarrassed me in front of her. How dare they tell me I'd made a mistake and punish me. It made me appear lesser than them and weak, which, ironically, was how I felt. Using magic usually imbued me with an intoxicating rush of power; instead, a wave of weariness washed over me. The curse had sapped my strength.

Sitting down, I put my head in my hands and considered what to do. In order to free myself from Ulika, I had to find the sand devils, and in order to do that, I had to go deep into the desert and lose myself again without using magic. But how to defeat them? If I could trap them again, that would solve the problem, but I needed to bait them. The gods had rejected my request for help, and discussing my plan with Ulika was futile. She didn't know I was the one who'd set them free, and I had to keep it that way. I didn't want her to look at me with panic and disappointment, the way she'd looked at Justice. Besides, despite this ordeal, I'd have the one thing I wanted. Her.

Ulika lay on her side, her head propped up under her elbow. Sleep softened her worries and fears, but the lamp sat between us, a stark reminder of why we were together again. This was no blessing of fate, much as I wished it to be. I had to be careful lest I fall under her spell. It had been difficult enough to leave her the first time. The second time would be torture. Unless she no longer returned my affection for her; I hadn't considered that only because I'd never seen her with another. The idea of her falling in love with a mortal, marrying him and having his children, sent a lightning bolt of rage through my heart.

Ulika mumbled under her breath and then sat up with a start. When her brown eyes met mine, behind them was a hollow longing that made my chest ache. I stood, suddenly feeling self-conscious about what had happened in the hall of the gods and my unhappy thoughts regarding our lack of a future. When I spoke, my words came out rougher than I intended. “We should go,” I told her.

10

ULIKA

We were back. I jerked awake, hoping it had all been some terrible nightmare. The shape of Vinn sitting across from me reminded me it was no dream. My throat was thick with the truth. He was the god of wind. I'd experienced his magic and power for myself, except now he appeared diminished somehow and also embarrassed.

Vinn was the god of wind. I had to toss out everything I'd assumed about the gods and about him. I was getting my wish, but he was forced to help me against his will. My veins hardened with dread. This situation was not how I'd imagined it to be. I thought I'd walk into Fae Mountain, I'd offer the lamp as a gift, and the wind would whisk across the desert and destroy the sand devils all within one rising and setting of the sun. Instead, I'd learned the truth about Vinn, trapped him, and taken away his free will. In the mountain, he'd almost begged the goddess to set us free, as though he resented what had happened. As though he resented me. I couldn't fall apart in front of him. I had to keep my resolve, pretend he meant nothing to me, because it was clear I meant nothing to him.

"We should go," he suggested.

I nodded in agreement. I had to show him I was willing to work with him, to make this easier for both of us. "Go where?" I asked, standing.

"To hunt the sand devils. I know where they dwell. All we need to do is find them."

I raised my eyebrows. He was ready to get started right away, but he sounded so sad. Questions rushed into my mind. "You make it sound simple. Do you believe it will take three months?"

"It might. I am uncertain how long it will take to traverse the desert on foot."

I straightened. "I have my camel, Nika. She's tied up just outside. At least, I hope she's still there. She has a tendency to wander off."

A flash of amusement crossed his face. "I still have never ridden a camel."

The softness in his features reminded me of old days, when I'd thought he was mortal like me. Something inside of me softened, and the pain in my heart lessened somewhat. I knew something a god didn't. "I'll teach you. It's easy," I offered.

"Listen." He ran his long fingers through his unruly hair. "About what happened back there..." He cleared his throat. "Are you okay?"

I stared at him in surprise, and something between a snort and a sob rose in my throat. I pushed down that emotion because I had to be strong. He was Vinn, but he was an immortal god. The gulf between us widened because I was only a mortal, as the goddess in the mountain has said repeatedly. It would be easier if he were indifferent or hostile, but kindness would shatter me. "I was prepared to sacrifice myself if needed, but you should know I'll do whatever it takes to complete the task the gods have given us."

His face went hard, and he moved to the ledge.

Snatching up the lamp, I hastened after him, confused because there was a sense of warmth and camaraderie followed by a cold tension. Why had he asked that question if the answer angered him? Was it because I'd mentioned the gods?

The silence stretched between us until we were outside in the blazing sunshine. It was hot and bright, and relief flooded me, for Nika was still tied up, munching on dried grass. It was only with a pang I realized what I had to do. Facing Vinn, I announced, "We have to return to my tribe. I want to tell my family goodbye."

Vinn moved to Nika's side and scratched the side of her neck. "Is that wise?"

My words came out in a rush. "I don't know how long our journey will take, and I don't want them to worry. I only planned to be gone for a morning."

Vinn nodded. "Ulika, how do you intend to explain my presence at your side?"

I chewed my lower lip as I studied him. Taking Vinn back to my tribe carried some risk, for we only had three months together. No more. After he conquered the sand devils, he'd return to his life as the wind, and I'd return to my tribe. It would be wiser if we went straight into the desert right now. When I reappeared three months later, no one would know what had happened. But I couldn't imagine doing that to my family. They'd worry, search for me, and assume the sand devils had killed me. I could not inflict that grief and sorrow on them.

Vinn's second question broke through my thoughts. "How would you react if someone told you they'd brought the god of wind to help them fight sand devils? Would you believe them?"

"I..." My lips were dry again, but his intense stare made me self-conscious about licking them. "I suppose."

He shook his head, making his tousled hair dance. "No, there's a reason I never shared the truth about who I am. I've watched many from above, seen their actions, listened to their conversations. Yes, I know more about mortals than you would imagine." He tented his long fingers together, a sudden hardness crossing his angular face. "Mortals are full of words, but they don't truly believe in the gods, or have faith in them. Do yourself a favor and don't tell them who I am."

I frowned, crossing my arms. "I can't lie to my family."

"Who said anything about lying?" He drew closer, a finger resting on my shoulder as mischief flitted across his face. His voice dropped as he added, "We are bound together. At first I was angry but the gods are correct: I should have stopped you from entering Fae Mountain. But it was you, and I was astonished and curious as to why. I've never seen you travel so far from your tribe. Tell them I'm returned to marry you. And then we'll leave."

With each word, he drew closer. Dumbfounded, I tilted my head to stare up at him as he invaded my space. He'd returned to marry me. Could I sell that story to my family, my tribe? It would be easy. I tried not to let my gaze linger on his broad shoulders, his naked chest, or his arms bulging with muscles. But I couldn't ignore the way his hand rested on my shoulder, for it was comforting and hinted at something sensual. His dark-brown eyes darted to my lips before his gaze bored into mine. The idea bloomed before me, marred by what had happened last time. He'd left me before, and he would do so again. I jerked away, crossing my arms over my chest as though that action would protect my heart. "This is my tribe, my family. I care about them and what they think, and you have no one and nothing."

My harsh words made him flinch. He stepped back and squinted at me.

I brought my hands up to stop him. "I didn't mean it like that, only we don't have everlasting life like you. This small moment in time might seem insignificant to you, but to me, it means everything."

He turned away from me, and I twisted my fingers together. I'd said the wrong thing. Why couldn't I hold my tongue?

"It's true, I don't have what you have, and it might appear that I have nothing, no one I care about," he said, his voice rough. "But I have power and immortality, and if I help you, the spirits of Val Ether will give me blessings. So you see, there's something in this for both of us. If you wish to go to your tribe, we will go, and I will be your husband, as the gods commanded."

A thread of doubt snaked through me as Vinn turned to Nika. She knelt, allowing us to mount, and we started across the desert, back home.

II
VINN

When the white tents of the camp appeared, I slid off the camel's back. Ulika looked down at me, a quizzical expression on her face as she tugged on the reins. I hadn't wanted to see this ruin of her people, or feel the guilt that slithered through me. The once clay homes were gone, replaced with scattered tents. Even though the campsite was by the river, they'd moved further south to where caves jutted out of the ground, providing shelter against the wind.

The caves were damp and wet—unlike my dry mountain—with nothing more than bats and beetles. Now and then I'd seen a glint of light, as though the walls hid jewels, which wasn't uncommon. Occasionally, a tribe stumbled across a stream of gold, or found diamonds in the sand. It was rare, but the desert held treasure, and the idea of it was tempting. But what would I do with treasure?

An undercurrent of despair and dejection hovered over the camp, and it was quiet, with only the indistinct murmurs of conversation. The cry of a young child occasionally split the air and then, in the distance, the sound of a stringed instrument being played. The air was still, and that was when I recalled my winds could no longer blow across the desert.

I crossed my arms as Ulika dismounted and gathered the reins. She'd mentioned that one of the sand devil attacks had stolen most of their livestock. All but a few camels remained.

"It's different from when you were last here," Ulika explained, leading the way into the camp. "Do you hear the music? Each afternoon when the sun is hot, the bard sits by the river and plays. The water carries sound so all in the camp can hear it. It's healing, helps soothe the children, and during the hottest part of the day, we usually sleep."

I fell in step with her. "So everyone is sleeping?"

"Not everyone. Usually someone keeps watch up on the rocks." She pointed, then waved at a figure in the distance.

Sure enough, someone sat in the shade of the rocks over the caves. They waved back, but I couldn't make out any distinguishing features.

A moment later, a whirl of white hurled toward us, and a young woman launched herself into Ulika's arms. "You're back. Finally! Did it work?" When our eyes met her grin widened. "Vinn! You've returned."

Anat was a younger, shorter, more petite version of Ulika, impatient and full of chatter, with a restless energy.

"I've come to help," I explained.

Anat clasped her hands together. "With the sand devils? Ulika said she was going for help, but I didn't expect you. She was going to Fae Mountain..."

Ulika raised her hand. "I'll tell you everything later, Anat. Please don't pester Vinn with questions. He's our guest for tonight."

Anat wiggled her eyebrows. "Lucky for us we just had a big catch of fish, even though I'm getting sick of eating fish. Ulika, come to the tent. Mama and Papa will want to see you. It's been almost a full day since you left."

I watched the interaction, wondering if I should walk away and leave them to discuss. There were undertones and nudges in their speech, another reminder of what I lacked. Touching Ulika's shoulder, I gestured toward the river. "I'll go listen to the bard. Find me when you're ready."

Her eyes went soft with gratitude. "Thank you."

I appreciated her words, but it only made me feel more alone. Like she'd said, the camp was quiet. Most tent flaps were open, the inhabitants hoping for a cool breeze while they slept, and I passed families deep in slumber. The sand devils had attacked these people, and I didn't need to hear their stories to know what had happened to them. The gods had sent me to make their lives easier, and instead I'd failed.

The waters sparkled by the bank, and I sat down under the shade of the palm tree. Ulika was right; the music was soothing, and as I sat, watching the fish swim mindlessly under the surface, an idea bloomed.

12

ULIKA

Vinn walked away, and I wished he hadn't gone, even though I sensed he was giving me time to speak privately with my family. But we were in this mess together, and he'd left me to deal with it alone. It was too late to call him back as his muscular form disappeared around a tent, leaving me alone with Anat. She pinched me, grinning with excitement. "You found Vinn! I thought he was gone forever. Explain!"

Twisted emotions made my throat thick. I was happy he'd returned yet upset about who he was. I need more time to process what was happening, but there was no time. Squeezing Anat's arm, I kept my voice low. "Where are Mama and Papa? I need to speak to them, and I'd rather tell you with them."

Anat's eyes narrowed, but she slipped her arm in mine. "Ulika, what's wrong? I thought you'd be happy that Vinn returned. I know you like him. What did he do? Did he hurt you? I'll take Papa's spear and drive him away."

I squeezed her hand. "Vinn did nothing wrong. Please be patient. I'll explain."

Anat was never patient, nor could she stop talking. It was no surprise she wasn't asleep at this hour. She barely slept at night, waking up every few hours to whisper her dreams to me. Still, she was loving, was protective, and had a way of cheering me up. Suddenly, I hugged her. Tomorrow I was leaving for an unknown amount of time, and I'd never been away from my family.

The big tent in the middle of the encampment belonged to my parents. Each person in the tribe had their work, but my parents were skilled in finding old relics, and my Uncle Noah was in charge of trading with each tribe. He was a jolly man, full of stories, or at least he'd used to be before the sand devils had attacked. Now he sat up on the rocks above the cave, keeping watch and whittling wood into crude weapons. Weapons made us feel better, even though they were useless against the sand devils. Who could fight the wind except the god of wind himself?

Anat burst into the tent, where Mama sat cross-legged on a rug, polishing jewels, and Papa shaped clay into vessels. Anat got her restless energy from them, for their hands were always busy.

"Ulika!" Mama exclaimed, dropping her cloth. "Where have you been? It's been a day and night since you disappeared. We thought you'd been kidnapped, but Anat said you went to Fae Mountain. Is this true?"

Papa squinted at me, taking in my appearance, and then pointed to a rug. "Sit, eat, then tell us. All that matters is that you're home safe now."

Weariness overcame me as I sank down. Papa passed me a plate of flatbread and crushed beans with spices. I'd forgotten about food during my adventure with Vinn, now I ate quickly, my eyes heavy with sleepiness when I finished. Anat's never-ending chatter floated to my ears. "She came back with

Vinn, but he wasn't wearing a shirt or carrying a pack. We should give him some clothes."

Clothes for Vinn was a good idea, but I wished Anat hadn't brought it up, because suddenly Papa was staring at me, his lips turned down with displeasure. As a patient man, he'd reserve judgment until I shared my side of the story, but all the same, my stomach turned sour. Why had I eaten so fast?

"We'll discuss Vinn in a moment, but going to Fae Mountain is forbidden for a reason," Papa said. "Care to explain?"

I fumbled with the scarf around my neck. The gods had seen fit to return the cursed treasure to me, and slowly I unwrapped the lamp.

Mama gasped. "Where did you find that?"

"Do you know what it is?" I searched her dark eyes.

"It's a lamp, a golden lamp. If the trade routes were still open, my daughter, you could have anything you desired."

Tears clouded my eyes as the truth burst from my lips. "I found it a few weeks ago, and I know I should have shared it, but I wanted something special, just for myself."

"Oh, Ulika," Mama tutted.

"I would have done the same," Anat added, bouncing on her toes as she stared at the lamp.

She was just trying to make me feel better; she would have done no such thing. Anat couldn't keep secrets for very long. An hour later, she would have blabbed the news about the lamp to everyone in the tribe.

I continued, "Then the sand devils came and...everything was awful. I decided to use the gift as a sacrifice for the god of Fae Mountain. So I went, and it turns out, this lamp is cursed. Anyway, I found Vinn, and he returned to..." I couldn't say the word *marry*, so I moved on. "We came to an agreement: he's going to stop the sand devils, and I'm going with him."

"Vinn? A mere man is going to stop the sand devils?" Anat exclaimed, and then a laugh burst out of her lips. "You're joking, right?"

Papa raised his hand, motioning for her to be quiet. "Ulika, is this true?" he asked, his tone calm and even.

I nodded, repeating my words as though that would make them true. "He's going to get rid of the sand devils."

"Praise be!" Mama exclaimed, lifting her hands. "I'm not sure how much longer we can dwell with the fear of an attack."

"You're not joking," Anat breathed, collapsing on a rug, wide-eyed.

Papa was not done. "Why are you going with him, Ulika? What are you not telling us?"

I took a deep breath and said the words in a rush. "We're going to be married."

Anat's eyes went wide, and then she squealed. "Married! Congratulations, Ulika."

Papa stilled, and his eyes narrowed. "So quickly? He only just returned."

"Hush," Mama whispered. "Married, what a beautiful thing. We've needed a reason to celebrate, and Ulika has brought us two."

I wished Vinn had come with me, to appease my papa, who stood, his jaw set. "Where is he? I'm going to have a word with him. Leaving like that so long ago and then appearing to demand my daughter's hand without talking to me!"

Anat, who loved drama, leaped to her feet. "I'm coming too."

"Papa, please be kind. This is what I want," I begged, a surge of determination strengthening my voice. "Tomorrow he and I will go into the desert, defeat the sand devils, and return. I'll only be gone a little while. It's a small price to pay for freedom."

Papa shook his head. "I don't like it. Let me have words with this Vinn. To marry you and then want to take you into danger? It's wrong."

I opened my mouth to protest again, but Mama shook her head. "Ulika, you've had an ordeal. Take a nap, rest." Her gaze fell on the lamp, and she stared at it before shaking her head. "You'd better hide that. If it is cursed treasure, we need to get rid of it."

Papa and Anat swept out of the tent, leaving Mama and me alone. I wrapped the lamp back up, while Mama moved to the tent entrance. "I'm going to find you something to wear tonight. Sleep."

I wanted her to stay, to speak more about what had happened, but she slipped out of the tent, leaving me in silence. Pressing my lips together, I lay back and let my secret burn within me. I'd dreamed of the day I'd meet Vinn again, but not like this, and now we were to be married. How much of this ordeal could my heart take?

The sound of laughter woke me, and I startled upward. I was still in my parents' tent, and daylight had faded. Stretching, I noticed the clothes Mama had laid out for me. A white dress and golden circlet to go in my hair. Clothes fit for a wedding. My skin flushed hot as I went to the basin and wiped down my arms and legs. I brushed my hair until it shone and then dressed. Too bad the sand devils had smashed the looking glass. Leaving my hair loose, I pulled my scarf around my shoulders and ducked out of the tent.

No winds blew tonight, and most of the tents had been packed up and stored in the caves in anticipation of another attack. The caves were cold at night with a bite of dampness that left the older and younger ones—more susceptible to disease—coughing. This evening, though, no one had gone to take shelter in the caverns. Instead, they were by the riverbank. Was there going to be a wedding after all?

Trying to shake off the sense of unease, I hastened toward the merriment. Music played, drums beat, fire had been lit, and people danced around it. Aimee, one of my close friends, whirled around with her husband. She'd gotten married the year before and was pregnant with her first child. Uncle Noah perched atop a rock with a group of children surrounding him. They shouted and shrieked, leaving me to assume he was telling a story of his adventures.

Anat whirled around the fire, long arms in the air, her skirts twirling, while Jadda, the oldest member of my tribe, mixed dye from a henna tree and painted it on arms and legs. The dye helped cool our skin from the heat of the sun, and Jadda claimed the designs she drew were fortunes. She'd be upset that I was getting married without one of her fortune-telling designs inked on my skin.

The rich tang of cooked fish made my stomach growl. We'd had fish and beans and flatbread for days on end since trade had dried up. It was only recently that Uncle Noah had found a supply of spices that hadn't been ruined. We had little, but I was proud of my tribe for working together without complaint.

I scanned the gathering, searching for Vinn, a mix of emotions roiling within me. I wanted him, but I wanted him to want me too. My heart beat faster when I located him, dancing around the campfire. Someone had given him a shirt, and he blended in as though he was one of us. Yet there was something about him that stood out and attracted us all. His presence had drawn us under a spell. A god was within our midst.

I searched for Mama and Papa, who were going to have words with him, words I feared would lead to some kind of negative consequence. Instead, they sat under a palm tree, sharing a drink. A knot tightened in my belly; this was happening.

Suddenly, Vinn towered over me, grinning recklessly. His stoic demeanor had vanished, and he smelled of spices and fire. A light shone in his deep-brown eyes as he looked me over. "Ulika, you look well rested and beautiful."

Firelight glowed on his bronze skin, and all resolve to harden my heart against his charms melted away.

Stepping closer to him, I kept my voice low. "Vinn, did you speak with my parents?"

"I did." The smile did not leave his face, but he studied me for a reaction as he continued, "You told them we are to be married and then go into the desert to vanquish the sand devils. Your father is quite fearsome." He chuckled. "I had to make all kinds of promises to appease him."

I glanced at the bank where my parents sat as though they didn't have a care in the world and then to the rocks above the cave where no one was watching for an attack. "What did you do to my parents and my tribe?"

Vinn put a hand over his heart, trying his best to look wounded. "You underestimate me. I know the hearts and minds of your people. Most want to hear my story and know where I've been all this time, and they wanted a reason to laugh again. When the weight of the world crushes you, don't you want a night of celebration? A reason to escape? It helps you forget instead of wallow in your fears and grief. Our union is such a night. Come, Ulika, marry me, dance around the fire, forget about the future, and enjoy the moment."

As he spoke, he took my hands in his, squeezing them gently. Under the starlight, it was easy to smile up at him, my heart fluttering with hope. I shouldn't fall for his magnetic smile or the spell of his charm again, but I wanted to. Just for tonight, I'd forget about impossibility and, as he said, enjoy the moment, before we went into the desert and everything changed.

Tomorrow, when the sun came up, I'd remember that Vinn was the god of wind, he'd left me once, and he'd do so again. But he was here, right now, and my heart surged under the weight of his attentions. My nod was all he needed, and he pulled me toward the fire.

13

VINN

I married Ulika, daughter of sand, that evening. The voices of her tribe lifted in song and laughter, making my spirits light. Ignoring the warnings that rang within my soul, I focused only on that moment and the fact that I was no longer alone. She was beautiful, dressed in white, with a gold circlet woven into her hair. The pain of parting was gone, and when she smiled at me, I thought I'd drown within her soulful brown eyes. Perhaps gods weren't meant to be alone, without the love and respect and worship of mortals.

Earlier, I'd been sitting on the bank with my feet in the water, watching the silver fish nip my toes. Her papa had stormed toward me, furious at me for leaving, then returning to take advantage of his daughter's innocence.

The truth flowed naturally from my lips. I'd left because I wasn't able to give her what she wanted, but I'd returned because of the sand devils. I admitted that I cared about her, and spoke of the future. Not the hopeless future of Ulika and me, but the future of the tribe. If her papa misunderstood, that was his fault.

Safety and security were most important, and with the sand devils gone, they'd have freedom once again. I spoke of Ulika's passion for painting and Anat's bright spirit, how neither of them should be trapped in a cave. Freedom was most important, and their spirits would thrive once I had cleansed the desert. I told him he was the leader of the tribe and had to protect it. The people were weary and disheartened, but a celebration would boost their spirits.

He'd warred within himself but had eventually conceded I was right and given me his blessing.

Jadda spoke the words of the wedding ceremony, wishing us a long life (I already had that), blessings (I'd ensure Ulika was wealthy), and many, many children. I banished the brevity of three months from my mind, recalling my advice to Ulika to enjoy the here and now. We feasted and drank and danced.

When the velvet shadows of night fell, a chill descended, making the warmth of the fire particularly enchanting. I attempted to hold Ulika in my arms, but she squirmed away, gyrating to the beat of the drum. The people of the desert did not dance in slow and seductive movements like the fae. They danced as though their very lives depended on it, a breathless, demanding dance, legs kicking, hips shaking, hands and arms briefly intertwining.

Ulika laughed as she danced, and her lightheartedness was so enchanting I was tempted to kiss her. My pulse throbbed with yearning, for the wall of distance between us was gone and this might be the only time she might accept me as her husband. My heart thudded in my chest, an unusual sensation, and wind stroked my hair.

I didn't notice it the first time, but the second time, I stilled. A sulfuric undertone hung in the air, and the wind blew steadily stronger. I caught Ulika's arm. "Quick, to the caves."

The joy on her face died in an instant, and she spun around before whirling back to me. "Tell the musicians. I'll warn the others."

She dashed off, pulling people aside and whispering in their ears. Impressed by her calmness, I hesitated, but when the strength of the winds returned, I moved.

Moments later, a horn sounded, and the tribe surged toward the caves. The music changed from merriment into a thump of drums, a warning rolling through the camp. My moment to save Ulika's tribe and vanquish the sand devils had come, but all too soon.

The wind roared, hurling sand at me. I closed my eyes, reaching for the magic that was locked within. I could not let the tribe see the sand devils defeat me. Wind alone would not stop them, so I stepped into the river and pulled the waters to me. They came with a roar and wail, but the goddess of the river yanked back, chiding me against stealing her waters.

I had forgotten she dwelled there and promised to return every drop that had been taken. I'd speak to the rain and ask it to replenish her waters. She relented, and I turned back to the shore. Flames from the fire licked the air as though nothing was wrong, but the horizon was black with streaks of violet lightning. The wind howled as a cloud rose out of the desert, a vortex thundering down upon the tribe.

Readying myself, I watched, surprised as I made out red eyes, pointed horns, and a jagged shadow. A deep voice bellowed, and suddenly I understood why the tribe called them sand devils. These were not natural creatures but things made of shadows and darkness, coming to take what they desired. Not tonight. I pulled the strings of my magic and hurled myself toward it.

14
ULIKA

"Where's Vinn?" Anat asked as we huddled together in the cave.

The walls shook as the storm outside wailed. A baby cried, and I squeezed my eyes shut. The howling made me want to cover my ears and scream and scream until it stopped. But I didn't have the excuse of being a child. Instead, I tugged Anat closer, my lips trembling as I spoke. "He's seen the sand devils before. He'll know what to do."

I only prayed my words were true.

"I'm glad he returned," Anat whispered back, her words just barely audible over the roar of the wind.

"You were really sad, and now he's going to make you really happy."

A tear leaked down my cheek, but I did not brush it away, for Anat would notice my movements. Instead, resting my head against hers, I nodded. She didn't know it was only for three months, and I hated to consider how I would explain myself when I returned. Alone. He was the god of wind, and we had no future together. The wedding ceremony had only made a flutter of hope burn within, a flame I needed to extinguish now. Vinn was only playing a part, but if I wasn't careful, I'd believe that he cared for me after all. Had I been wrong about his indifference toward me?

The windstorm continued, hushing us into silence as we waited in the dark. Vinn was out there, facing the monsters while I cowered inside, helpless. An irritating thought wormed into my mind. What if he defeated the sand devils tonight, lifted the curse, and broke the bond? My fingers trembled as I recalled leaving the cursed lamp in my parents' tent, where it was likely getting buried by sand. It was probably for the best. The lamp should be melted down, destroyed, so that no one could use it again.

We waited for an indeterminable amount of time until the wind stopped and the terrors of the night morphed into a peaceful silence. Gray light filtered into the cave, displaying shadows and hunched forms. I blinked against the darkness and kept my face pointed toward the entrance, willing Vinn to appear.

Part of me was torn, hoping for the ordeal to be over but not wanting Vinn to leave. Earlier, the wedding I hadn't wanted had ended up being exactly what my people needed. The joy, the laughter, the food and dancing without worry had momentarily wiped our troubles from our minds. And Vinn, how was it possible that he was the god of wind? If I hadn't seen his power for myself, I was unsure if I'd believe it. Tales had led me to believe gods were powerful, arrogant, angry, and impatient with mortals. But he was none of that.

I closed my eyes again, because when Vinn and I had been dancing around the fire, a look in his eyes had made me believe he might kiss me. That was the problem. I'd questioned his affection for me when he'd left, and again when we'd been in Fae Mountain. But now? It shouldn't matter if he returned my affections, because what I desired was not possible.

Besides, if he defeated the sand devils tonight, he'd leave, and then what? I'd go back to my life—finding treasure, painting—and one day, find a new husband. But I had to admit to myself that even though I should be grateful, I wanted more than the life I had.

It wasn't until sunrise that Papa deemed it safe to leave the cave. Untangling myself from Anat, I crept around the sleeping bodies and out into the pale morning light. Papa walked beside me, and Uncle Noah had already taken his place on the rocks above. Hues of blush covered the sky, the first signs of a riot of colors.

"By the gods," Papa breathed.

I dropped my gaze down to the desert floor, and my eyes went wide. The landscape of the desert had changed. Dunes curved around the encampment in a half circle, leading to the waters. The pale-pink hues of the sun made the sand glitter like gold. My mouth dropped open, but only one word escaped.

"Vinn," I breathed and darted down the pathway to the shore.

The encampment should have been in ruins. Instead, the fire had been built up again, unlit but ready for another night of celebration. Something silvery glinted on it, and my parents' tent was standing as though the wind hadn't happened at all. I broke into a run, tearing inside, where the bundle with the lamp lay. I picked it up, my heart thudding in my chest as I raced out of the tent and made my way to the river. He was gone, wasn't he? Why did my chest hurt?

I ran past the bonfire, noting the sparkling items on top were fish, dozens of them, as though the river had emptied itself on top of the shore.

There, under a palm tree, sat a man. No, it was Vinn. He only looked like a man, the glamour of a god even further diminished. This was the second time he'd used magic. For what else could explain what had happened? Suddenly shy, I slowed my pace, but he rose.

"Ulika."

"Vinn?"

He approached, a raw look on his face, one that I couldn't quite decipher.

"Are the sand devils gone?" I asked.

His gaze went to the river, and he shook his head as though he was ashamed of himself. "No, I frightened them off and built a barrier of sand to keep your tribe safe while we are hunting. We need to leave before the trail goes cold."

15
VINN

White sand swelled into tiny dunes and opened into scattered paths criss-crossed with both human and animal footprints. Ulika and I were not the only travelers in the ever-changing desert, especially in the early morning. Hares scurried to their dens, sand foxes trotted by, and beetles scuttled across the desert floor before burrowing deep into the dust. By midday, the sun beat down with a relentlessness that made me grateful for the head covering Ulika's parents had gifted me with. A wedding gift, as they'd called it. I didn't have the heart to tell them this sham of a marriage would be long over before I saw them again.

When Ulika had come to my mountain, she'd claimed she was willing to sacrifice herself to save her people, but I doubted she was aware of the true cost. Last night, before the sand devils had ruined the celebration, she'd been happy, in contrast to this morning, silent and still. She sat rigidly in front of me, and the way the camels' humps swelled allowed us to ride without touching. It was slow and even, and as I scanned the barren horizon, impatience made me itch. To distract myself, I tried to get her to talk. "Do you still paint?"

Ulika shook her head, black hair swishing back and forth down her back. "Not anymore. During the first attack, my jars were crushed, and with everything in chaos, its selfish to spend time making dye and enjoy a frivolous activity."

I frowned at the reminder of my guilt. "Your paintings are lovely, not frivolous."

Ulika shrugged but kept her face forward. "True, but my time is better spent helping my tribe. We have to work twice as hard to find food, store our supplies in the cave, and remake what was lost. I feel selfish taking time for myself when I could help others."

Of course, fighting for survival meant work. I'd forgotten, again, the difference between us. "You work hard. Surely you'll take some time for yourself."

She shrugged. "When this is over, I will."

But there was a catch to her tone, a distinct note of unhappiness, so I shifted the topic. "Once, I flew over the southern lands, and the people painted their pots with various dyes. Before they dried, they baked them in the fire. The paintings crystalized and formed unique designs and patterns, making them more valuable for trade. And no one admonished those who painted for taking time for themselves, for they were both creating and giving back to their people. You could do the same."

Ulika gave a soft sigh. "You're right. Will you tell me more of your stories? They were my favorite. I always wondered how you traveled so far and wide and appeared so young, but knowing your divine nature brings clarity." She sounded so wistful when she spoke.

"You want to travel too, don't you?"

"I've heard marvelous tales my entire life, of cultures with traditions different from my own, lush lands with green gardens, and trees taller than the cacti. I long to see the birds with bright feathers and hear their songs as they fly across the sky. One day, I'd like to see beasts as big as a boulder and flying lizards who breath ice and fire."

"Who told you these stories?" I asked, for I hadn't told her all of them.

"Jadda tells stories while she paints fortunes. I've worked alongside her all my life. She also told me about gods in their heavenly homes, bringing down wrath upon the mortals who displeased them. In her tales, gods are powerful, arrogant, easily angered, and unforgiving, yet you are none of those things. Even when we went to the hall of the gods, you were not like them."

Her praise made my heart swell, and suddenly I understood why some gods dwelled among the mortals and demanded their worship. Praise from their lips was like a sweet elixir. I didn't know how to tell her that, or if I should mention how her words made me feel. Wasn't it a weakness to rely on the praise of mortals? Instead, I offered something safer, a glimpse of my past. "No, I didn't grow up around them, nor am I as ancient as they are. I'd rather live in this world than sit in cold halls above."

"Do they truly sit in cold halls? What do they do?"

"They amuse themselves watching the world, making predictions regarding the future, and bickering."

Ulika giggled. "Bickering? Gods bicker?"

"They do, sitting on their lofty thrones, believing themselves better than everyone else because they have everlasting life and a higher intellect. I'm young, but still, the idea of it, lifetime after lifetime, it's as endless as the sand. So much time to live often leads to mischief and misdeeds."

"You're mischievous, aren't you?"

I feigned innocence. "What makes you think that?"

"You're the god of wind, and you've blown across this desert, perhaps my entire life."

Her entire life. I didn't like the reminder of my agelessness but said nothing about it.

Ulika continued, "The wind is always mischievous."

"Helpful?" I offered.

She glanced back at me, eyes lidded. "It was you, wasn't it, the time I dropped Papa's scrolls? I tried to gather them up, but you sent them flying across the campsite, and I had to chase them all down. And there was the time I spilled my paints and you hurled them into the tent. There was an inky black splotch until Mama replaced it. I have more stories, proof that you are mischievous."

I burst into laughter, and after a moment, she joined me, her low, throaty giggles making something twitch deep inside. "Admit it: if not for me, your life would be dull and boring."

She playfully swatted at my arm. "No, it would simply be incident-free. I have enough excitement in my life without your winds adding to it."

"Do you?" My voice came out harsher than I intended, only to mask my true feelings. She'd dropped her guard and was having a candid conversation with me, just like old times. "I very much doubt that, or you wouldn't have fetched me as your personal guide through the desert."

Just like that, the carefreeness between us sizzled. Her shoulders went tight, and she faced forward again. When she finally spoke, her voice was low. "There's more to this world than sand and dust. I'd love to see it the way you see it."

There, that was her true wish. To see what I could see, to go where I'd been, to experience the joys of a lifetime. Impulsively I touched her shoulder, half turning her to face me. "When this is over, I will show you the world."

A half smile came to her lips. She opened her mouth to respond, and a wall of sand washed over us.

16
ULIKA

Vinn was flirting with me, just like he had in the past. A bloom of warmth filled my belly at his attention, even though I shouldn't welcome it. I had to keep distance between us because this was temporary. I couldn't grow used to his intriguing conversation and deep tones. It was wrong to even entertain the idea that anything could happen between us again.

And then something shot out of the sand. I cried out in surprise and yanked on the reins, forcing Nika to break into a trot. But the thing was faster. A whiplike tail slammed into Nika's side. Vinn and I tumbled into the dust, and I rolled, coughing and gasping as Nika struggled to regain her feet. I lunged for her and snatched my father's spear off her back. He'd given it to me as a parting gift. Even though he did not want me to go, he understood it was the only chance we had.

A high-pitched cry sent shivers up my spine as my fingers squeezed the solid wood of the spear. The tail disappeared into a cloud of dust. Shielding my eyes with my scarf, I coughed, unable to see Vinn. I hoped he wouldn't use his magic again, because we'd barely begun and he'd already used it twice. How difficult would it be to cross the desert without magic? Surely other tribes did on their journey to the river.

Silence descended, and just as the dust settled, a blur of motion came at the corner of my eye. I ducked and pressed myself against the ground as something wide and luminous crept over me. It had claws and an arched tail, and with a shout of determination, I thrust the spear forward. The bones in my arm jarred as my weapon connected with something hard. A crack came, followed by a wail. Pain rushed up my arm, and my vision swam. I'd hit something. Hard.

My fingers loosened around the spear, and then a firm hand was at my back. Vinn. His fist closed around the spear, and he pulled it free, then thrust again, just like I had. Another sickening crack came, followed by a cry of frustration. The sand whirled around us as the creature spasmed in its death throes, and then there was silence.

Vinn wrapped an arm around my waist to steady me as we caught our breaths. It was another few moments before the dust cleared, and by then, the pain in my arm had settled into a dull ache. I stepped back, breaking the contact between us as I shook sand out of my dress, my hair, my scarf.

Vinn prodded the exoskeleton of the creature with the bloody spear, while Nika trotted off to a low-lying bush and started chewing on it, as though she hadn't just been knocked over by a giant scorpion. At least, I guessed that was what the creature was, with two pincers, a curved tail, and green blood that glowed in the daylight.

"Careful, the blood might be poisonous," I warned Vinn.

He finished his examination and returned to my side. "You were quick, and good with the spear. I've never seen a creature this size. Is your arm…" He trailed off.

"I'll be fine. The shell was harder than I expected, but the spear went right through it. Have you seen anything like this during your flights across the desert? It looks like a scorpion but bigger than the ones I've seen."

Vinn scratched his head. "It is unusually large, and it came right up from under the sand as though it was hiding and we stepped on it."

He broke off abruptly and stared across the desert, thinking.

I wondered what his thoughts were and if he was drawing the same conclusion I was, that the strange creature had appeared because of the sand devils. Something had disturbed the balance in the desert, and darker creatures were coming forth. I glanced back in the direction of my tribe. We were barely a half day's ride away. What if there were other monsters headed toward them? I hoped Uncle Noah was vigilant in keeping watch and would keep them safe from the unknown.

Suddenly, flirting with Vinn seemed pathetic considering the situation. We had a quest that would mean life or death for my tribe. I did not have eternal life to fall back on when everything went wrong. Hiding the lamp was supposed to be the beginning of a change, for Papa forbade me to join Uncle Noah on one of his trading trips, which was why everything I'd done had been in secret. Now I was paying for it.

Without another word, I sprung up on Nika's back and clutched the reins. "We should go," I told Vinn, my tone sharp. "We have a long way to travel, and if more of these monsters are coming out of the desert, we have to stop them."

17
VINN

Three days passed, and the desert shifted as we traveled deeper into it. I'd never noticed how scorching hot the sun was during the day and the stillness that crept across the air without my winds to blow down from the north. The nights were cool, and in the wasteland of the desert, it was even colder and lonelier. When I'd stayed with Ulika's tribe by the river, there had been fires, but more for cooking than for warmth. Now the idea of the friendly orange flame would be comforting in the dark coolness of night.

Each evening, we set up a small tent and ate flat-bread and cold beans under the starlight. Ulika was withdrawn, often rubbing her shoulder even though she claimed she wasn't injured. By all appearances, she wanted to be left alone. The void between us was chilling, and to give her space, each night I offered to sit outside the tent and keep watch. I listened to the howls and cries of the nocturnal creatures, some finding food, others unlucky enough to become a larger predator's next meal.

Nights were cold and dark and full of terror, along with the hovering of a menacing presence, as though the desert plotted against me. Even more concerning was not knowing when the sand devils might attack again.

The third night in the desert, I sat on a rock while Ulika slept in the tent behind me. The long, weary nights made me wish I could blow my winds across the desert. Sleep was uncomfortable. When I closed my eyes, a sense of unease came over me, as though something was watching, waiting to take me off guard. The slow-moving journey tried my patience. I wanted something to do with my hands, whittling wood, shaping clay, anything but pouring sand through my fingers and watching while the camel slept. She was the most passive creature I'd ever met. Nothing upset her.

The tent flap opened, and Ulika poked her head out. There was just enough moonlight to let me see the shape of her body and the white of her teeth when she spoke, but not much else. She rubbed her arms as she joined me on the rock. "It's chilly out here. Aren't you cold?"

I shrugged. "It's the same as it's been every night. Why aren't you sleeping?"

Ulika tucked her feet under her and gazed up at the starry sky peppered with silver streaks. "On nights when I couldn't sleep, I'd lie by the river with Anat. The sound of water is soothing, like a lullaby. We'd watch the stars and see how many constellations we'd find. I always thought the sky would look different if I traveled, but it's comforting to know that whenever I go, it's the same sky, same moon, same stars looking down at us." Her voice sounded wistful and lonely, and I glanced at the tilt of her chin, the way she stared up as though searching for answers.

"When I left the Frost Mountains and came down here, it was comforting to see something familiar. Except the sky is much further away and without the trees and mountains, it appears bigger."

"What was it like coming from the land of ice and snow to here?"

"It felt like freedom."

Her head dropped, her gaze firmly fixated on me. "I...have a question, and if it is too personal, you don't have to answer," she said.

Now it was my turn to face her. "Ask," I encouraged.

"When we were in Fae Mountain, before you took me to the hall of the gods, I touched you and had visions of a beautiful place, crisp, cold air, lush gardens. Just flashes of it. Was that where you lived before?"

"You saw all that?" I exclaimed, unable to hide my surprise. "Is this the first time it has happened?"

Twisting her fingers together, she nodded. "Do you know why?"

I studied her. How odd. My thoughts returned to Val Ether, and Justice holding tightly to Ulika's hands as though she could sense something about her. I'd been angry and frightened the gods would discover how much I cared about her. Now, as I thought back, I recalled it was only after Justice touched Ulika that she pronounced she would not dissolve the binding. Was it because she'd read something in Ulika and guessed that in order to defeat the sand devils, I needed her? Justice claimed Ulika had no magic, but what if some other power was awakening within her?

Moving closer, until our knees touched, I placed my hands palm up. "I don't have a logical explanation, only an inkling."

She gave a sharp intake of breath, and her voice was soft when she asked. "What do you think it is?"

"Close your eyes," I instructed, taking her hands in mine. "Tell me what you see, or feel."

Her fingers closed gently around mine. Everything about her was soft but hiding surprising strength—like the way she'd slain the scorpion, or at least wounded it so I could kill it. She attempted to hold me at a distance yet treated me with reverence. She was a mortal, forbidden, but all the old feelings were resurfacing in her presence. Instead of leaning in, I should tell her to go back inside the tent and go to sleep while I sat outside alone, reading the future in the stars.

Ulika's voice brought me back to the present moment. "I don't see anything clearly, just a blur of green and red flowers, like the ones you had in the mountain. I get the sense of a lush, beautiful land, and it smells delicious, and yet...something is wrong."

Ripping her hands out of mine, Ulika opened her eyes. The way she looked at me made my heart beast fast. What had she seen?

"Vinn? Did something happen in the Frost Mountains? Did someone force you to leave and come here? I know you said you were assigned, but...it didn't feel that way. It didn't feel like a choice."

My heart closed, and a hardness came over me. But I didn't want those emotions anymore. They had always left my side of the story unsaid. Perhaps she was the one willing to hear the truth, and not judge me like the gods.

18
ULIKA

I laced my fingers together as Vinn spoke, because what I'd seen was potent as though I'd been there.

"I was young once, and yes, I know what you're thinking. I'm a god. But I was much younger than I am now," Vinn began. "I grew up among the fae, and in my youth and immaturity, I was arrogant, rather boastful about my unique skills, and as you mentioned earlier, mischievous. Magic is common among the fae, but many were jealous of my power. They were attuned to nature, had beautiful gardens where all plants thrived, and tamed monsters. But not the wind. Never the wind.

"One day, the son of the king and I were battling to best each other with our powers, a friendly competition, but a child crossed our path, and our magic killed him. The king took us to Val Ether for the gods to judge us. The gods took the king's son to live in their halls, as though that would be punishment. But to me, they gave the harsher edict because I was a god. They sent me where no one else wanted to go, to the wastelands of the desert. They believed it was my fault, but it was an accident. It was, and is, never my intent to harm any living creatures. But that is my shame, my lesson from the past. Each time I see a child, I strive to make them happy, and the rosebush I took from the gardens of the fae is a reminder that one must endure thorns to find what is beautiful."

A lump swelled in my throat. His story, and the knowledge something had wounded him, made me feel closer to him. It made him seem more mortal. What had happened was a defining moment in his everlasting life, and he'd chosen to share with me. "I'm sorry that happened to you," I said, taking his hand in mine.

This time, the flashes I got were of warmth and desert. As though by sharing his tale, he'd freed himself from the earlier memories of lush lands and death.

"Are you happier? Now that you're here," I asked.

I meant the desert, but he mistook my meaning and squeezed my hand, his voice dropping to a husky tone. "I'm happier now that I'm with you."

He was flirting again, reminding me of days of old when I assumed he was mortal like me. Shadows of sorrow squeezed my heart. But he wasn't leaving today. When he was gone, it would hurt, but each moment with him I'd treasure. "I did not know that gods could suffer. I assumed everything was well, but what you've told me has shown a different side of your character."

Vinn turned my hand over in his, tracing the lines on my palm. "Mortals are flawed, and having a god in their midst brings out the ugliness within them. Like a mirror reflecting what they cannot attain. The gods of Val Ether decided it would be better for gods to be alone, above all mortals. But mortals were not created to be alone, so why should gods be?"

Something inside me twitched as his fingers moved over my skin. For all his might and strength, he was lonely. Why hadn't I seen that before? Ignoring the warnings within my soul, I rose. "It is cold outside. Come sleep in the tent, and I do mean sleep."

He gave a low chuckle. "My dear wife, I understand this is temporary. I have no dishonorable intentions."

Wife. Right. We were married, but he had not chosen to exercise his marital rights. I pivoted away from him, because when I held his hand, I sensed something else from him: a desire with intentions that were very dishonorable, and in my weakness, I wanted him to act on those desires.

Rubbing my shoulders, I offered an excuse to explain my actions. "It's chilly at night and even colder out here because we're alone. I'm used to sharing a tent with Anat, and we don't have the warm bodies of the tribe and livestock to keep the warmth in."

Vinn touched my arm. "You don't have to explain. I'll keep you warm. I must admit, I'm pleased you asked me instead of Nika. She probably would have rejected you, being the most passive animal I've ever met. Does nothing bother her?"

Laughing at the idea of snuggling with Nika, I poked him in the ribs. "She smells. I don't know the last time she took a bath. The stink of her in the tent is not worth it."

He laughed too, and the sound sent warm vibrations fluttering in my belly. "Speaking of, we should find water soon."

"I agree. Our food is running low too. Mama only packed enough for five days, but you know the paths of the desert."

Vinn did not reply immediately. Rubbing the back of my neck, I bit back my next question and used reasoning to reassure my growing concern. As the god of wind, Vinn blew across the desert daily, and his knowledge would help us find the sand devils. Right?

"We'll figure it out in the morning. The desert has always given to those who need."

"That hasn't been my experience," I admitted dryly. "But perhaps you will change my luck."

When he did not reply, I tilted my head back for one last look at the silver stars and the pale light of the moon glowing far away in the night sky. Shadows moved, and again came a bead of fear. I was alone in the expanse. Shivering, I opened the tent flap. When I peered back, Vinn was right behind me, and suddenly I was nervous at what I'd asked of him.

The tent flap let in little light as I lay down on the rug. A moment later, he was beside me and my fears evaporated. The previous two nights, I'd shivered in my thin clothes while he'd sat outside, and my fears had kept me from asking until I was reminded of words of wisdom Jadda had shared. *Sometimes all you need to do is ask the gods. The worst they'll say is no and you'll be no better off than you were before. But what if they said yes?*

Vinn slid his arms around me, pulling my back against his chest. "Warmer?" he murmured into my hair.

"Yes," I whispered breathlessly, wondering if he would be so bold as to try anything else.

I may have imagined him kissing the back of my head, and that was the last thing I recalled before I drifted into a dreamless sleep.

19
VINN

Ulika slept soundly in my arms all night long, but I got little sleep. I breathed in her scent, for just holding her made me ache. I'd missed her. Joy filled my chest because she'd let me in. Our physical proximity only mirrored the connection we'd shared under the stars. Her presence eased the rawness of my soul, and the hushed warnings of the future became nothing more than distant whispers. There in the tent, I held on to one truth. We belonged together.

My mind raced. I had to find a way for us to be together, and I didn't think she'd need much persuasion. I was the one with eternal life, and if I was careful, took her on trips, showed her the world, and ensured we never lingered in one place for too long, we might have a chance. Oh, but if the gods found out, there would be hell to pay. I turned the problem over and over in my mind all night long, without a final solution.

At sunrise, we continued on our journey, swaying on Nika's back while we traveled further into the desert. Ahead and behind me, everything appeared the same. Day four and we were no closer to finding the sand devils or any clues to where they'd gone.

Ulika was in lighter spirits. She told me stories of her tribe and a temporary peace enveloped us, as the barrier between mortal and immortal vanished. I let myself forget about the complexities of a future and what the gods would say when we completed our quest. All that existed was the here and now, and I would enjoy it for what it was. Except the desert was determined not to let me forget.

Just past midday, an odd winking in the distance caught my attention, but Ulika was the one to draw the camel to a halt. "Look!" She pointed. "See that fissure in the desert? It's like a line, a zigzag split. Should we follow it?"

I swung down, eyes narrowing at the clear path that cut across the sand. It was just a line, a tiny crack in the ground, but already my mind went back to the hole where the sand devils had sprung out of the desert floor. Squinting at the light, I stared again at the glimmer in the distance. Taking the reins, I led the way, following alongside the path.

Four days and the sand devils hadn't attacked. I puzzled around it but couldn't figure out why, unless once a week, they rolled across the desert, seeking tribes to attack. That or they were summoned, pulled by magic. The magic of the lamp.

"There's something ahead I want to study," I called over my shoulder. "A winking in the distance."

"I think I see it too," came her soft reply.

A few moments later, the light became more than that, a gray shape rising out of the stone. It pulsed with a greenish hue. A rune stone. I'd never seen it during my flights across the desert, and an uncanny sense of premonition came over me. I stilled, while Ulika swung off the camel, and together we stared up at the rock. It was seven feet tall, the rune glowing like a beacon.

"Have you seen anything like it?" Ulika breathed.

"No."

"It's magic, isn't it?"

"I believe so," I agreed. It rose like a signal, pointing the way. "It's an omen, a clue. We are going in the right direction."

20
ULIKA

The jade rune pulsed like a heartbeat, keeping rhythm with mine. The longer I looked at it, the more a fevered heat spread through my body. My fingers tingled and even though the air in the desert was dry and still, whispers drifted to my ears.

Go back, daughter of sand. Avoid the curse. Return to your land.

I startled. Those whispers had begun when I'd gone to Fae Mountain. Try as I might, I couldn't shake the feeling that something deeper and more complex than I understood was happening. Perhaps when I'd found the lamp and captured the god of wind, I'd unearthed something. I pivoted to Vinn, trying to keep the panic out of my voice. "What is this? It feels like a magical warning or barrier. Will you explain?"

He crossed his arms but didn't meet my eyes. "I know as much as you know, Ulika. I've never seen this before."

A tick of irritation left me due to the sense that even though he wasn't lying to me, he was hiding something. I frowned. "You're the god of wind, of this desert. You're all-seeing, all-knowing."

"Ulika."

Taking my wrist, he pulled me closer until I was forced to tilt my head back to get a clear view of his face. We'd been close last night, but with the darkness, I hadn't seen him clearly. Now the broadness of his shoulders, the warmth of his hand on my back, and the way his eyes softened as he looked down at me sent my pulse throbbing. He was devastatingly handsome, even without his shroud of power. His pointed ears and the perfection of his form were the only indications that he wasn't mortal. At his touch, my breath came short, my mind spinning back to last night and the way he'd held me, gently, tenderly, as though my comfort was the only thing that mattered. It hurt to look at him because the desire on my face was impossible to hide, and it wasn't one-sided either.

"The desert is awakening. The gods of Val Ether warned me that it has something to do with the lamp. It is a powerful magic, but it is cursed. The sooner we are free of it, the better."

"The lamp," I repeated. His words gave me a reason to pull away from him and catch my breath again. Fumbling at the bundle tied around my waist, I pulled out the lamp. "So this is my fault?"

"Don't," he said hoarsely, raising both hands and stepping back. "I have no wish to be trapped in there again."

I replaced the lamp and tied the bag shut. Just a moment ago, we were close enough to kiss, but now I took a deep breath to steady my nerves and ask the question burning in my mind. "But you're confirming the lamp is evil and the sand devils came because of it?"

"Other factors are at play, but it is one reason the desert is awakening."

The lamp was to blame. My limbs trembled as I recalled the first attack and the way my tribe had run screaming to safety while the relentless winds had crushed everything. My actions had accidentally done that. I snatched at Nika's reins so Vinn wouldn't see how his words affected me. It was my fault for finding the lamp, being greedy, and wanting something all to myself. Look what it had wrought.

"Don't blame yourself," Vinn said, reading my thoughts just as easily as if I'd spoken them aloud. "You couldn't have known what the lamp was; only a god would have recognized its power."

"Did you not see?" I begged, tears in my voice as I climbed onto Nika's back. I wanted someone to blame, to take the guilt off my own shoulders. "You're the wind, all-seeing, all-knowing. Did you not see me find it? Why didn't you warn me?"

He did not respond, and my frustration only grew. This was why we were bound together, to teach us some kind of lesson, but what if I was the sole one to blame for this? I dared not look at Vinn as he mounted up behind me, and my shoulders stiffened when he tried to touch me. Let him feel what it was like to be human, to suffer, to have guilt, to regret one's actions and have no recourse.

Silent tears slipped down my cheeks along with an iron determination. If the sand devils could be killed, I would take up my papa's spear and slay them all.

We hadn't gone far when Vinn reached around me and yanked on the reins.

"What are you doing?" I snapped.

He swung off Nika and dragged me to the ground, where I stood fuming in front of him.

"Don't be angry," he pleaded. Threading his fingers through my hair, he lifted my face to his. "Mortals have opinions of gods. It helps to inspire fear and worship, to put a barrier between mortal and immortal. But I'm here because I'm on your side. You asked for help, and I gladly give it. We will go into the desert, find the sand devils, and break this curse, and you will return to your people victorious. You came to me, remember? Do I not have your trust?"

I did not answer him for three reasons. The first being that he was right: I was the one who'd asked for his help.

The second being that flashes of fragrant lands rushed before me, greens and reds and the chilly winds of mountain peaks.

And the third being that he kissed me.

When his warm lips brushed over mine, gentle, hesitating, I froze in shock. Vinn was kissing me. I'd longed for this moment for months, dreamed about it. But it wasn't Vinn the mortal, but Vinn, the *god of wind* who was kissing *me*. A mere mortal.

Shock faded into desire, and my fingers fisted around his shirt. I pulled him closer until his chest pressed against mine, and opened my mouth. He tasted like purity and magic and strength, everything I hoped and desired promised behind the power of that kiss. I moaned into his mouth and tilted my head, pressing against him for more. I wanted more than his essence; I wanted all of him.

21
VINN

Instead of claiming her mouth with mine, I should have apologized and told her I had a share in the blame. She might have found the lamp, but it was I who'd unleashed the sand devils across the desert. But she was already upset, her brown eyes swimming with tears, and I couldn't stand the thought of her crying, so unhappy. Even more so if that anger was directed toward me, as it would be when she discovered the truth. If she asked more questions, eventually the truth would come out, and instead of letting that happen, I did what I'd wanted to do for so long. I kissed her, and it was better than anything I'd experienced.

For a moment, her entire body went rigid, then her soft lips parted, and she kissed me back with a heat and passion that made me feel as though I was drowning. Her lips, her tongue thrusting into my mouth, her warm body pressed against mine, awoke a desire that had long lain dormant. I wanted her; I wanted companionship and connection. A deep need rose, and suddenly I didn't want to lie, to hide the truth from her. I wanted her to know me, to see me truly.

She was shaking when I broke the kiss, her fingers tight around my shirt as though she would rip it off. I stroked a finger down her jaw, and when her eyes met mine, they were deep pools of desire. I wanted to take her then, right in the sand with the blistering sun glistening on us and no one around for miles. Out of the corner of my eye, a darkness loomed on the horizon. Storm clouds?

Resting my hands lightly on her shoulders, I told her the truth. "It was me. I set the sand devils free."

Ulika's face crumpled as though I'd punched her in the stomach with the butt of the spear. She ripped herself free of my touch, spun on her heel, and ran.

My shoulders sagged as I watched her go. She hadn't asked any questions or waited for me to explain. She'd just run. I picked up Nika's reins just as a sharp wind blew. There, in the direction Ulika had fled, a darkness crept toward us. The sand devils were coming in the middle of the day, and I could only use my magic once more. I scanned the barren land for shelter as I leaped onto the camel's back. Urging her into a run, I dashed toward Ulika.

22
ULIKA

It was him! I panicked and ran because I couldn't think of anything else to do. He'd freed the sand devils, which was probably why the gods had forced us to complete this quest together. Both of us were to blame; that was the truth he'd hidden from me and that secret taste like a lie, even though the gods couldn't lie. Was it possible there were two sides to Vinn? One was the storyteller I'd fallen in love with, and the other was the god, a trickster full of mischief, willing to play with the hearts and minds of mortals.

After all, he had kissed me, and that kiss had answered the call of my heart, the longing to be seen and desired by him. I wanted him to desire me as badly as I yearned for him, but longing clouded my judgment. I wiped my lips with the back of my hand, but the taste of him was imprinted on me. When he'd kissed me, I'd sensed a cave was nearby and something evil haunted the wind.

"Ulika!" Vinn shouted.

Wind whipped away his words, and only then did my vision clear. A wall of darkness rose in front of me. Wind. But not *his* wind. A storm. I jerked to a stop. My hair twisted as though a hand was yanking at my scalp. Sand swirled, and I jerked my scarf over my nose and mouth as a muscular arm bore me upward.

Vinn hauled me on top of the camel, yanking me tight against his body. So tight I couldn't breathe. The last thing I wanted was to be in contact with him again, not now, not after what had just happened, but there was no time to fight. The wave of darkness coasted toward us. I snatched the reins, and shouting at Nika, who finally noticed my sense of urgency, I drove her toward the cave.

Blood roared in my ears as the storm drew nearer. We weren't going to make it. There was too much open space, too much sand. Visibility lessened, and grit stung my bare legs, driving beneath my skin. Vinn leaned over me, his hand sliding around my waist, and for a moment, I feared he would use the last of his magic to whirl us free of the storm. Instead he pulled, and we tumbled off Nika's back.

I wheezed for breath, but Vinn grabbed my hand and dragged me through the storm until the ground opened up and everything stopped. I scrambled to untangle myself from Vinn, blinking as I took in our surroundings. We'd slipped into a cool recess underground, and the opening above us let in glimpses of the storm and a steady stream of sand, flowing like a miniature waterfall.

I pressed myself against the cool stone, waiting for my heartbeat to return to normal. We were safe. For now.

A faint silver glow came from the rocks, displaying the angles of Vinn's sharp cheekbones, highlighting the fact that I was alone with him until the storm passed. I couldn't ignore him or pretend the kiss hadn't happened. It had. I'd enjoyed it. But that was before I'd known what plagued my people was his fault.

"Those aren't sand devils," I said. "It sounds like a sandstorm."

"You're right," Vinn said, a hesitant note in his tone. "Ulika, we should talk about what happened."

My shoulders went stiff. "We don't have anything to talk about."

"Yes, we do," he replied firmly.

"No," I half whispered. How I wished none of this had happened and I was back by the river, with my family. I wouldn't hope, wouldn't dream of one day traveling the world, running away and seeing something besides sand and cacti and white desert flowers. I'd dreamed too big, been too bold, and this was my punishment for stealing a lamp and wanting to change my future.

"Ulika, you should know what the gods told me."

When I didn't respond, he continued, "They believe the sand devils arose for two reasons, the first because the lamp was found, and the second because the barrier that kept the sand devils out of the desert was broken."

"And you did that," I said, accusing him of the crime he'd confessed to.

"And you trapped me in that cursed lamp," he retorted, drawing closer.

"I didn't know what I was doing," I shot back.

"Neither did I!" he rebutted. "A pile of rocks in the middle of the desert looked like they needed to be knocked down, and then those infernal creatures blasted me away before I could put them back."

I paused, my anger fading somewhat. "You mean they bested you?"

He grunted. "They surprised me is all. I wasn't prepared for what they'd unleash on me."

"And that's why you weren't able to defeat them when they attacked my tribe? You were there. You used water and created the sand dunes when you're not supposed to be using magic."

"It wasn't the right time. They have to be returned from whence they came. I just couldn't let you blame yourself when it was the consequence of both our actions."

I stared at him, the dreaded truth sinking in. The cursed lamp. The freeing of the sand devils. "It still doesn't explain the scorpion, nor the sudden sandstorm."

"No." Vinn's fingers curled around mine. "But we'll figure it out, together."

"We have no future together," I said bitterly, to mask the shivers that went up my spine at his touch. It was impossible to be angry with him. "You're a god, and I'm a mortal. When you defeat the sand devils, this will be over. We'll go our separate ways—"

"I know," Vinn interrupted, a raw note in his voice. "I don't want this to end either."

My lips parted at the shock of his words, making me slow to react when he leaned in to steal another kiss.

23
VINN

"Vinn, don't," Ulika breathed.

She pressed her hand firmly against my chest before I could steal a kiss, her wide brown eyes studying my face in the low light. I sensed her anxiety and trepidation. She was torn between two worlds, but so was I. Instead of persisting with the kiss, I covered her hand with mine, leaning back slightly to give her space to breathe. To decide what to say next.

"We don't work," she said at last, dropping her head. "This moment is but a short space of time, especially in your lifetime. The thought of death has made us cling to emotions of the past, bringing us together when it's better if we stay apart. The gods were not happy with us. Do you believe for one moment they will allow us to be together? Do they know you presented yourself as a mortal and visited my tribe?"

"No, and they will never find out. They are already unhappy with me, hence our current predicament. But I don't care what they think, and you're wrong about clinging to emotions of the past. I left because I didn't know how to show you who I am, and I can't be torn, pretending to be mortal when I am who I am. Even now, walking on the flat lands without the wings of my wind to speed our journey is a cruel punishment. But my feelings for you haven't changed, despite the rising and setting of the sun, even though I left and tried not to watch you or your tribe. Somehow, someway, I was always pulled back to you, as though an invisible rope tied us together. I don't think it was a coincidence that you found the lamp, climbed my mountain, and trapped me with fire. Something is changing within you, and I don't know if it's magic or something else. All I know, Ulika, is that I don't want to lose you again, and this time, you see me. You know the truth of who I am, where I come from. I know my past, but I want you to be my future, and if I must, I will fight the gods to ensure I stay by your side."

"Can you? Can you really?" Ulika begged, tears in her voice. "You truly want me? I don't even know what a life by your side would look like!"

I cradled her cheek in my hand, enjoying the feel of her smooth, soft skin. She leaned into me, her featherlight breath fluttering over my wrist. "A life with me would fulfill all your dreams. We'd travel, as you've always wanted. I'd show you the snowy mountains, take you to the fields of golden poppies and down to the more populated kingdoms where magnificent palaces are built of stone. We'll travel far, but we'll always return to your tribe as long as you wish it, especially when we have children. We'll find treasure, silver and gold, and the trade routes will flourish again."

Ulika gave a gentle cry, and I pulled her against my chest, holding her close as I'd wanted to do for so long. This was where she belonged. It didn't matter if she aged faster than me, for an end comes to all things. But the time I had with her would be the most important. We were single-minded in focus, and what might be seen as a curse was actually a gift from the gods.

"Vinn, you make it sound so easy, almost too good to be true."

"Because loving you is as easy as breathing. I've never stopped since the day I left."

"I love you too," Ulika confirmed, then she drew down my head and kissed me.

24
ULIKA

I only woke because it was silent. My head was nestled against the crook of Vinn's neck. The steady rhythm of his heartbeat had lulled me to sleep, along with the confession of love. Vinn had held me all night long, his arm firmly around my waist. Aside from kissing, we'd done nothing more. But my heart was light, and happiness surrounded me.

A sense of determination filled me as I sat up. There was nothing we could not conquer. Together.

My ears rang from the sudden silence as I moved to the entrance. The opening above me let in a tiny stream of golden light, and the pile of sand at my feet made me realize just how bad the storm had been. With a pang, I recalled Nika. She had everything. Our food, water, the tent, the spear...

If we were stranded out in the desert without her, we wouldn't survive long.

"Vinn," I called, spinning around, but he was already awake. My heart flipped at the sight of him, unruly hair, open shirt, and bare feet. He looked comfortable, at home no matter where we camped.

He pulled on his sandals and paused, one finger in the air. "Do you hear that?"

I frowned and craned my neck back up at the opening. A low boom echoed, steadily growing louder. "Sounds like drums," I told Vinn as he joined me.

"Let me go first," he cautioned, hoisting himself out of the cave.

A moment later, his hand came down, and he helped me up.

I squinted against the blinding sunlight and raised my hand to shield my eyes. The landscape had changed. Sandstorms often whipped across the open desert—another reason my tribe kept to the river—but I had never experienced one for myself. Now my jaw dropped at the swells of sand, the stunted bushes blown over, and—somehow, someway—the cacti that lined either side of the cave entrance, standing firm as though they'd never let the wind knock them down.

The quick look was just enough time to show me that Nika was nowhere in sight, but a group of people marched toward us, playing the drums. They were a small group, men and women, even a few children, dressed in bright colors, hues of red and yellow I'd never been able to accomplish with my paintings. Each one had a drum around their waist, likely made from wood or clay with an animal skin dried and stretched tight over the opening. They pounded with their palms, and the sound wasn't that of celebration, as it was when my tribe played the drums. Instead, it was a hollow warning, and something stirred within me, as though these people were going to war.

"Have you seen them before?" I whispered to Vinn.

"They are one of the many tribes that roam in the center of the desert. I've always wondered why. Maybe they haven't found the river yet."

“I mean, are they friendly?” I asked, thinking of Nika and how we needed something to trade for more food and water. Or perhaps they’d seen her.

Vinn shrugged, and I guessed he did not make it a habit to visit tribes and determine if they were peaceful people. It was too late to question him further, for one man waved at us. He must be the leader, for the drumming stopped, and he approached.

He was about the age of my Uncle Noah, with thinning black hair, round cheeks, and a paunch that spoke of many nights of indulgence. He wore a linen shirt and trousers, and kicked up sand as he moved toward us. “Oy! You there! Did you come out of the cave? You killed it, didn’t you?”

“Killed what?” asked Vinn.

My brows knitted as I studied the man, weighing his question.

“The monster?” The man gestured to the hole in the ground. “We’ve been waiting for weeks for it to die or for someone to slay it. Natural springs flow underground where it dwells, the only source of water for my tribe. Every sunrise we come here, playing the drums, hoping to scare it out of its hiding place. It's already eaten three of my warriors, and the sacrifices we bring won't appease it. Surely, tell me, you slayed it."

I glanced at Vinn, for we hadn't seen a monster. Perhaps the howl of the wind had kept the monster from finding us, if there was one hidden deep in the caverns. "Nothing attacked us last night," I told the man. "Nor did we explore the caverns. But we'd be willing to make a trade if you'd like us to check." My cheeks flushed with pride at how naturally the words left my tongue. Was the power my uncle carried when trading? "The sandstorm surprised us, and we lost our camel and supplies. If we ensure the monster is dead for you, will you give us food and water for our journey?"

The man stared at me, rather slack-jawed, then glanced at Vinn, who was just as surprised. "Your wife drives a smart bargain." He winked, then stuck out his hand. "I'm Leban, and you have yourself a deal."

25
VINN

"Why did you make a bargain so quickly?" I asked Ulika as we climbed back down into the hole.

Leban had given us two torches, a spear, and a bucket for water. I eyed the torches tentatively, for ever since what had happened with the lamp, I had an aversion to fire.

"I didn't see any other way." Ulika shrugged. "We lost Nika, and we spent an entire night here without being bothered by a monster. Perhaps it's dead."

I chuckled at her optimism. She was happier, lighter ever since last night, and it warmed my heart to know that my choice to stay had brought her joy.

"It was smart. You're quick, but they are strangers. Why would you help them?"

"I'd like to think we are all affected by the sand devils in different ways. Maybe they haven't been attacked outright like my people, but remember the scorpion we killed on our first day in the desert? Perhaps this is a similar monster. Besides, it costs nothing to help, and we made a trade. Regardless of what we do, we benefit from this."

"It was selfless of you, and I admire your generous heart," I told her.

Ulika beamed at me as she held up the torch and led the way deeper into the cavern.

The walls widened, and the stone became slick with moisture. Presently, the scent of water became impossible to miss, along with a steady dripping sound. We slipped out of a passageway into an open space where a natural pool had formed. A shaft of light shone in from high above us, making the water shimmer. The walls also glowed silver, and I wondered if the tribespeople had ever noticed they could mine silver out of the rock. Was it better that they did not know? For often treasure led to disputes and trouble.

“There’s nothing here,” Ulika announced, walking into the space.

“Careful,” I urged her, gripping the spear. “Something might be hiding.”

She nodded and backed up a step or two while I stood by her side. Together we turned in a slow circle, searching for the alleged monster of the pool.

“Maybe it really is gone,” Ulika suggested, eyeing the pool.

She was thirsty. After all, we’d spent the night without food and water, and as a mortal, she needed the nourishment. Still, a thread of unease made me tense. Something was wrong here.

“Let me go first,” I said.

Putting down the bucket, I lifted the spear and walked toward the water. The pool was seemingly empty aside from the water. At the bottom, something glinted, a sizable chunk of gold, I thought, marred only by a spot of black in the middle. No. Not gold. An eye. “Get back!” I cried almost too late, as a monster sprang out of the water.

It was no river goddess but had the face of a horse, fishlike fins, tails like a lizard's, and claws. It was the size of a camel and lunged at me, snarling, and one word came to mind as I braced for impact. *Titans.*

When I'd freed the sand devils, I'd let something else out. Unusually large creatures, the titans of the desert, had come to claim it and plague the people. Ulika's tribe had sand devils. This tribe had a water monster. What else was wrong in the desert?

The water lizard pivoted at the last moment and slammed its tail into my torso. The impact knocked me on my back, and I let go of the spear with a grunt. That hurt. Instantly I wanted to light my hands and use magic, but I only had one chance left. The next time I used magic had to be against the sand devils.

Ulika was by my side in a moment, reaching for the spear. The torch lay on the ground, the flickering light poor as moisture seeped into it. It occurred to me as I regained my feet that Ulika had a better chance of killing the water lizard than I did. She was used to using the spear and light on her feet. She spun and stabbed before I could call her back, striking the underbelly of the water lizard.

It hissed in pain as she gritted her teeth and tried to pull the spear free, but it was stuck.

"Ulika!" I cried as the water lizard raised its claws and backhanded her.

She staggered back and landed with a grunt, and a whirlwind of fury grew inside me. It took all my self-control not to explode into a raging vortex of magic. Instead, I dived toward the lizard and yanked the spear free. It turned on me, growling, curved claws ready to tear me in half, but I would not give it the pleasure. We danced around each other, lunging and leaping, missing at every turn. Green blood oozed out of the monster's wound, and its progress slowed, allowing me the final blow.

I drove hard into its wounded belly, knocking it back. The lizard gave a high-pitched cry and scrambled back into the water. It fell, sending ripples splashing onto stone, and then, after a few twitches, it lay still.

Tossing the spear on the ground, I dashed to Ulika.

26
ULIKA

"I'm okay," I said as Vinn helped me up. "I just need to catch my breath."

He slid his arm around my waist, holding me close. "I didn't like that, the feeling of helplessness when the creature knocked you down. It made me realize how much I rely on my magic, while you use your wit and speed to take down a monster."

Worry made his gaze even darker, and to reassure him, I squeezed his arm. "But look, you slayed the monster without magic. That's the second time."

He grinned, then kissed my hand before turning to the natural pool. "Unfortunately, I don't think the tribe will want to drink that water."

Slapping a hand over my mouth, I giggled. "Did you have to put it in the pool? You couldn't strike the final blow against a wall?"

He pulled me tighter against him. "Dare you judge the god who slays monsters?"

I giggled again. It was refreshingly odd to have this experience with him.

"I'm glad you're not hurt," he murmured against my ear. "I suppose we should return before they think we're dead."

"There's still the problem of what to do about water." I pointed to the pool.

Vinn studied it for a moment. "Water is dripping in from somewhere beyond this cave wall. Perhaps the source is further in the cavern and flows to this pool. If we can find it, we can give the tribe uncontaminated water."

I nodded, and a question about whether it would be worth the extra time rose to my lips before I recalled we were not in a hurry. The time spent assisting the tribe would be to our benefit, and perhaps in the future, they'd become trade allies. They didn't know about my tribe or the supposed bad luck. "They'll want to know the monster is dead and see proof. It's likely they'll strip it down, use the bones for weapons, the skin and scales for clothing."

"Resourceful," Vinn mused. "Is that what all tribes do with the dead and forgotten?"

I raised an eyebrow. "We don't find monsters often, so we do what we can."

Vinn slipped his hand into mine, and together we left the cavern.

The tribe was ecstatic when we told them about the death of the monster, and everyone wanted to come see it. They were less upset about the water supply and encouraged by our generosity to help them find another source. I had to admit, it was good to be around people again, and for the first time in my life, I was surrounded by strangers. I wondered if this was what it was like for Uncle Noah when he went on his trading trips, not knowing what would happen but proud of the result and encouraged by the people he met.

Leban and his people swarmed the cave with torches, knives, and spears. They went straight to the pool of water and, after prodding the monster a few times to ensure it was quite dead, started skinning, chopping, and discussing whether the meat would be okay to eat. Soon they had pots filled and ran them back and forth from the cavern, back up to the surface.

Meanwhile, Vinn and I explored further, with the murmurs of the tribe and the cadence of their song echoing behind us. Eventually, we found a crevice in the wall where water dripped out with a slow and steady rhythm. We set a pot under it to collect the water, then shared a few sips before leaving it to fill up. Once we told Leban, he sent a few of his people to collect the water while they finished cutting up the monster.

“Look at them,” Vinn said, leaning against the cave wall, arms folded as we watched the activity surrounding us. “They are happy even at the prospect of having their watering hole back, and they are celebrating their success with their tribe. These are the kinds of things gods take for granted.”

I studied the museful look on his face, his expression I couldn’t quite read. “What does it feel like? Being part of this?”

“It gives my life purpose.”

Purpose. I considered that word as the day passed. What was the purpose of life? To live well, share experiences with loved ones, and bring joy to the people I met? But when I glanced at Vinn, a soft smile played around my face. The purpose of life was to love, as long as time would allow.

27
VINN

"Come back with us!" Leban announced, spreading his arms wide.

Behind him, one of the men carried the head of the water lizard, mounted on a pike. Its forked tongue hung out, thick and bloated, and its eyes were closed. The smell of it was sharp and pungent if one was standing in the wrong direction.

"You've saved us," Leban continued, "and we have that deal to make good on. We'll supply you with food and water as you continue your journey. I warn you though, the further you go into the desert, the more desolate it gets. What did you say you're after again?"

"Sand devils," Ulika spoke up quickly. "Have they attacked your tribe?"

Leban frowned and rubbed his jaw. "I haven't seen them with my own eyes, but scouts reported about some monster crossing the desert. A whirl of horns and wind and sand and red eyes, bigger than a mountain. I assumed it was gibberish. You know the desert can make you lose your mind. Too much time in the heart and one starts making up stories."

"It's no story," I confirmed, "and they are dangerous. Your tribe is lucky they haven't bothered you, but we're going to the place they come from to destroy them."

"Is that so?" Leban grunted. "Because of what you've done for us, I'd wager a few men would go with you and fight." He balled his hands into fists and punched the air.

I chuckled. "We'd be grateful, but these are supernatural beings like the water lizard. It's better if few lose their lives."

"No need to decide tonight." Leban waved his hands. "Come, let's go celebrate!"

The drums started up again, but this time, the thump was not in warning but a celebratory dance. Once again, Ulika and I were headed toward a feast, another victory, and I looked forward to it. In the future, I would spend my life as a half mortal, half god, knowing I'd always return to a tribe or from my travels with Ulika. Soon. I glanced at the sun hanging low in the sky. As long as the gods of Val Ether remained unaware of how I'd interfered with mortals against the gods' wishes, all would be well.

I recognized the home of the tribe when we arrived. A grove situated close to the cave, perhaps an hour's walk, no more. Tents made of skins set in a half circle dotted the area, but surrounding them were cacti—some ten or twelve feet tall—stunted bushes, and a group of camels and little foxes that trotted around, sniffing for animals burrowed under the dirt.

I'd blown past this tribe often, for they were clever hunters, more likely to trap animals with their ploys than actually slay them. Every few months, they moved to a new location. They were always hunting, always searching, and I wondered what kept them on the move, as though they couldn't find what they were looking for.

We strode into the middle of the circle, where the drums intensified, and I glanced around for the women and children. Something was off, odd about them. Usually they had smoldering remains of campfires, for they baked their food under the sand, a smart way to keep from roasting under the heat of the fire. Typically, the children ran around naked, playing with sticks and stones, shouting at each other or feeding the goats and camels.

The drums masked the sounds of their shouts and movements, but I couldn't help but sense something was wrong. The aura of magic made the hair on my arms stand up straight. Someone was here. Was this a trap?

The tribe surrounded us, and Leban stepped in front of one of the tents, opening the flap. "We've found them. Now please, let our people go."

Tallen walked out and a bolt of fury punched my gut. He had an elaborate way of playing with mortals, turning them against each other and giving the gods the upper hand.

He ducked out from under the flap of the tent, ax in hand, eyes cold. Beside me, Ulika drew a sharp breath, and he eyed her with distaste. I wanted to rip his eyes out of his skull.

"Vinn, so we meet again, only this time I've discovered that you violated the agreement you made with the gods."

My jaw twitched. For this to happen in front of so many mortals was unfair and his words utter blasphemy. I reached for threads of magic as I responded. "I've done no such thing. My actions have been in accordance with the word of Justice."

"I'm not talking about that agreement." Tallen shook his head. "I'm talking about an older one, a rule about what is forbidden, a rule you've broken."

I lifted my hands, but Tallen was faster. He brought up his ax, and I did not physically feel the blow, but suddenly I was trapped in darkness.

28
ULIKA

Vinn disappeared, and the half goat, half man, Tallen, grabbed me by the arm. I screamed, scratching at his furry arm, but he would not relent. The tribe cast their eyes down, ashamed by both their lack of action and what they'd done. What did it mean that Tallen was here? What would cause a god from Val Ether to make a trek to the desert and a deal with a tribe?

Bile rose in my throat, and my chest was tight as though stones were being pressed upon my heart. Tallen dragged me past the tall cacti, away from the tribe, and out into the middle of the desert. He did not stop until, when I looked back, the shapes of the tents had disappeared. Evening was falling though, and the sky was dusky when Tallen let go of me.

I staggered back, rubbing my arm, for his grip was bruising, and his height and breadth made the icy blade of fear slice between my shoulders. Clasping my hands around my stomach as though that action could keep me from being nauseous, I waited for him to speak. He was an arrogant god, and even an action I assumed was harmless might ignite his fury. Although, he was already angry with me.

Tallen frowned down at me, and when he spoke, his voice was deep and rough. “It’s not your fault, young mortal, yet you shall suffer for getting in the way of an argument with the gods. Vinn, the king of wind, is a trickster, and yet he coaxed you into loving him, did he not?”

I wasn’t sure if Tallen was asking a question or merely stating a fact, so I said nothing, my heart beating wildly in my chest.

“He made you feel special, like you were the only one who mattered. He promised to let go of his divinity and spend a lifetime with you, didn’t he?”

No, this could not be happening. Tallen spoke as though I was a victim, when it was easy to believe Vinn's words, his caress, his promises. I blinked, willing the tears not to come.

"It's happened before. With the fae, the mages, and now, out here in the desert with you. Each time, the gods punished him and told him to leave the mortals alone, but Justice was blind to the truth of what happened here. She didn't know that, long ago, Vinn spent time with you and your tribe. But I did, and so now I'm taking matters into my own hands. You are mortal. He is a god. There will never be a future between you. This is his last chance. If you care about him at all, when the quest is done, you will drive him away, or he will lose his divinity. Forever. I've done you a favor by trapping him in the lamp. Finish your quest, set him free, and then forget about him and go back to your life."

My knees wouldn't hold me. Clasping a hand to my mouth, I sank into the sand. Tears leaked out of my eyes like a spring rain, slow and steady. "How do I know what you say is true? And how will I complete the quest without him? He was my guide..."

I trailed off as a memory surfaced. When I'd touched him, flashes of a lifetime ago had come back, the perfume of flowers, a flash of red, but not of roses, of cloth, of all those he'd claimed to love before me. What did that make me? Nothing but a dalliance in the life of a god, a way to amuse himself as the time ebbed and flowed.

"I am a god. I cannot lie." Tallen snorted. He tossed something at my feet. "Take food and water, follow the line in the sand, and you will find the monsters that plague this accursed land. When you find the sand devils, and only then, rub the lamp, and he will appear to destroy them with magic."

I clasped my hands together. "Please, please don't do this. Break the bond. Let us go free."

Tallen lifted his mallet. "What is done cannot be undone. You must learn to live with the consequences you wrought, no matter how unintentional."

A flash of lightning lit up the evening sky, followed by a rumble of thunder. Tallen turned away as I folded into myself, my sobs coming thick and fast. I held myself tight as sprinkles of rain touched my shoulders, making my hair and clothes damp. Vinn was the god of wind, but he was so much more, and I'd let myself be led on like a fool. How old was he and how many lives had he lived before we'd met? I was just one of many, someone to love until he grew tired of me and left. Wasn't that why he'd left before? He'd done wrong in the eyes of the gods, laughing in their faces while taking what he wanted. I'd let him kiss me, hold me as though I was the only one, and disgust wailed up within me. I wanted to take the lamp and shake it until he came out, and I'd demand answers. It was so much worse only knowing the truth about Vinn from a god who thought ill of him.

But it was no use crying. Wiping my face with the backs of my hands, I decided to let myself grieve later. There were sand devils to slay, and I needed shelter from the storm. A bone-deep weariness came over me. Picking up the pack, I put one foot in front of the other while the rain poured down, a reflection of the pain in my heart.

29
ULIKA

Something nuzzled my head, and a wet and sticky substance licked the side of my face. I bolted upright, scrubbing at my cheek with the side of my dress, and gasped. "Nika!"

I threw my arms around the camel's neck, resulting in another rather disgusting lick and then a nuzzle as though she'd very much like to eat my hair. Pulling away, I patted her neck. "I'm glad to see you," I sighed.

The reins dragged on the ground, and all the supplies were gone, including my father's spear. But it didn't matter. Nika had survived the storm, and I wouldn't be alone in the desert anymore. After shaking the dust and sand out of my clothes, I climbed on her back and took in my surroundings. Last night I'd walked and walked but hadn't found any shelter. Then the night had swept in, cold and clammy, even now chills made my arms shake. My throat was raw, and my body ached. The cold and wet might have made me sick, or it could be the exhaustion from what I'd learned about Vinn.

I turned Nika west, and she set off at a steady pace, only too willing to be helpful to make up for disappearing on me. Vinn was right. She was the most uncaring beast and yet reliable all the same. Vinn. I had to stop thinking about him. My fingers gingerly went to the lamp, and I yanked them away. When I closed my eyes, I could see him as though he was standing in front of me, his heated gaze, dark eyes, and quick grin, and the way he had a habit of running his fingers through his hair. Worst of all was the memory of his lips against mine like a brand, the way he'd kissed me as though we were the only two people in the world who mattered.

I told my heart not to hope as I urged Nika into a trot, in a hurry to find the haven of the sand devils. Under the assault of Tallen last night, my heart had been broken, but once again, despite telling myself not to let it, hope bloomed. It did so much like the roses growing in Fae Mountain. Because they were strong and determined, they wouldn't take no for an answer, and they'd find whatever moisture they could in the rock and use it to make them stronger. The challenge of survival strengthened them, and I shouldn't take my lessons from the flowers, but my heart would not rest.

What if Vinn had fallen in love once and for all? He was a god, and he could not lie, leaving me to believe every word he'd spoken to me. If that was the case, who was Tallen but some taskmaster sent to keep the gods in line? That theory sounded laughable. For what was the point of being a god if you couldn't have your own way? If you couldn't go where you wanted, love who you wanted, and live the way you desired. That was the benefit of being a god, of having everlasting life, and yet Tallen's attitude made all my theories ring false.

Another worry plagued my mind. A line Tallen had spoken. If Vinn disobeyed the will of the gods again, he risked losing his divinity, which meant he'd be mortal, like me, and without the one thing that was important to him. Wind magic.

The truth dawned on me slowly and surely, like the sun creeping over the horizon. If Vinn truly loved me and wanted to spend a lifetime with me, he'd have to give up the essence of who he was. Wind.

It wasn't so much his divinity that he cared about but magic, which was why the goddess, the woman Tallen had called Justice, had given Vinn his task, as punishment to show him what life would be like, crossing the desert without magic. Perhaps she knew, had known all along, and believed this would be the ultimate lesson, the way to give Vinn a taste of what life would be like if he lost everything.

I weighed that thought, examining it from every angle. Was it possible? Then, if Justice—what an apt name—was omnipresent, why would Tallen travel from Val Ether to ambush us?

Vinn told me that gods had emotions, and when we entered Val Ether, Tallen had been the first to appear, to drive us away. He'd spoken of banishment, called Vinn a trickster, and remained angry, glowering in the shadows, while Justice had decided our fate. Why interfere with what the gods had wrought unless he had something to gain from it?

Wasn't that what Vinn had said? Gods were mischievous, brought on by their long life. What if Tallen had nefarious intentions?

Once again, I wished Vinn were not stuck in the lamp so that I could talk to him. He knew the way of the gods; perhaps the truth would be obvious to him. No matter what happened, Vinn had to keep his divinity, and we had to complete the quest.

I puzzled all day, while Nika obediently walked west. It was only when the shadows of evening grew long that I recalled I was supposed to follow the line in the sand.

Before me lay a crack in the ground, zigzagging away to the northwest. Mouth dry, I dismounted and ran my fingers over it. It was only a thin line in the dust, one that would steadily grow bigger as I followed it. Leading to what, more monsters and then the sand devils themselves? How I wished I had my father's spear or at least some knives from that tribe. But it was no use wishing for things that would not happen. Instead, I studied the ground. It was barren, dusty, hard ground without sand.

I'd reached the truly barren lands, where even the plants did not thrive under the harsh circumstances.

"This is far enough for tonight," I told Nika.

Not that she cared; she was already sniffing at a dried bush, trying to determine if it would be tasty enough to eat.

"I'm going to find some stones and make a slingshot," I went on.

The silence in the area was deafening, and the sound of my voice was small, dropping into the ground whenever I spoke. The sacred aura in the area reminded me of Fae Mountain. Shivering, even though there was no wind and the blazing sun was still beating down, I gathered stones, then settled down beside Nika for the night. She did stink, but I had no one else to keep me warm, and my chills from a night in the rain hadn't subsided.

Jumping at every little noise and wishing for a tent to protect me from the elements, I ripped my skirts and formed a slingshot. It had been a long time since I'd made one, and I practiced a few times, tweaking until it was just right. Feeling better about my safety, I piled rocks by my head and used Nika's side as a pillow.

Lying back, I stared up at the sky, expecting to see the stars winking down on me. But clouds covered the night sky, and I couldn't help but sense it was an omen of doom.

For three days, I followed the crack in the ground, and each day it grew wider, leaking fumes and leaving me with wild nightmares of what lay beneath the ground. Those were the three loneliest days of my life, for no animals lived out there, and vegetation was scarce.

Each evening, I collected more stones for my slingshot. Even though there was nothing to fight, having a weapon gave me a false sense of security and something to do with my hands. My swirling thoughts were my greatest enemy, and I spoke out loud to Nika often, to distract myself from the looming future. My night in the rain had made me sick, for sometimes my vision made me see double. I'd grow cold under the blazing sun and hot under the chill of night. Worst of all, my dreams were filled with memories of Vinn, when I'd known him as a mortal and then again as a god. I had so many questions to ask him when I was finally allowed to draw him from the lamp.

On the afternoon of the third day, a blur of shapes appeared in front of me. I pulled on the reins, and Nika came to a halt. Fumbling in my bag, I found the waterskin Tallen had given me. Despite how much I drank, or rationed, it never emptied, and I wondered if it was magical. And also why Tallen would help me. He'd appeared so fierce and angry, and yet perhaps I'd misread the situation. Still, something wasn't right, and I couldn't figure that out, so instead I should focus on the task at hand. The sooner I was back home, the better.

I swayed on Nika as I took a long draft of water. My throat was raw, scratchy as it went down, but at least my vision had cleared. The blurry shapes in front of me were stones, and I recalled Vinn admitting he'd knocked over a pile of rocks. I swallowed hard, which only made my throat hurt more. I'd arrived. It was time. "Nika, you need to wait here," I said, dismounting.

There was nowhere to tie her up, which meant she'd likely wander away again. The bag of rocks was too heavy to carry, so I selected five or six smooth stones and tied them around my waist, hoping it would be enough. Last of all I unwrapped the lamp and carried it in both hands as I made my way to the pile of rocks. They rose like a shrine, with green runes glowing on them. As I approached, the unearthly aura of them filled my senses.

Sweat made my forehead damp, the hairs on my arms stood up straight, and my breath turned shallow. I wanted to turn and run, but I reminded myself of my purpose. I'd come to save my people, to ensure the sand devils would leave this land forever. If this was the end, I had to be brave.

Beside the stones, a void opened up, and the foul smell wafted from it. I stared down at the hole in the ground and by sheer strength of my will, did not back away. I tapped the lamp. "Vinn, it's time for you to come out."

Nothing.

No, no, no. The gods hadn't left me alone to die, had they? In the barren wasteland of the desert where sand devils might attack any moment? I shook the lamp and with a heavy sigh recalled Tallen's words: *when you find the sand devils.*

Did I have to physically set eyes on them in order to get help? With a heavy sigh, I returned my attention to the void. I had to go down there in order to wake up the sand devils. Long slabs of rock led into blackness. With a curse, I made for them. Dirt and sand crumbled under my feet and I cursed. Shifting the lamp to one hand I loaded my slingshot in case I needed to smash something.

The sun let in enough light for me to see a wide-open, circular chamber. I paused halfway down, taking in the shadows hiding what I could not see. More monsters?

I tapped the lamp again. "Vinn, please help me."

Two red spots of light glowed from a far corner, and a low growl vibrated the air.

I took a step back toward daylight. "Vinn, I set you free," I whispered, fear making my throat thick.

The growl came again, this time a little louder, and those red eyes moved. Pointed horns appeared in the shadows, and my bravery melted like snow under a scorching sun. I spun around to flee, tripped on the ledge, and fell down, hard. My face scraped against stone, and a sharp pain sliced up my cheek. I cried out, struggling to regain my feet, and realized that I'd dropped the lamp.

But it was too late. Wind whirled around my ankles, and the dirt beneath me shifted. With a groan, I rolled onto my back. When I tried to put weight on my legs a stabbing heat flared from my ankle, forcing a cry from my lips.

A monstrous devil rose in the middle of the chamber, just out of reach of daylight but illuminated enough to display its true form. Horror crept over me. *Sand devil* was an apt name, with its red eyes, glinting horns, and shadowy face and body, shifting like the winds.

The ground trembled as it formed a vortex, and clawed fingers reached for me. A sob wailed in my throat, but I was frozen with terror. This was the monster that plagued my people, and it was foolish of me to think a mere slingshot might slow it down.

"Get away from her," a low voice growled. "Your fight is with me."

Vinn stepped out from where the lamp had fallen, and he was just as he'd been in the mountain. Wearing only a loose pair of trousers, his hands balled into fists. A flood of awareness filled me, and my fever returned. It was hot. So hot down there. But Vinn was here too; I wasn't alone. Except, we'd both die, because Vinn had admitted, the sand devil had already bested him.

30
VINN

Disoriented, I emerged from the lamp to shades of gray. The last thing I recalled was Tallen's ax slamming down. From the sea of blackness I'd drowned in, I'd concluded I must be back inside the lamp. But for how long, I didn't know. Time froze there; it could have been minutes, hours, days, or—I banished the next thought quickly—years. A muffled cry met my ears, and I cocked my head back, taking in the rough-cut slabs of stone and stairs, and Ulika, blood dripping from a gash in her cheek, sprawled out on them. Her eyes were wide in horror, only she wasn't staring at me but beyond.

Rough wind tumbled over my skin, and I turned my attention to what was in the chamber. Soulless crimson eyes bored into mine as the creature of shadow and death whirled itself into a vortex. Somehow I'd been transported to the lair of the sand devil, but I had no time to enact my plan and create a trap for the malevolent spirit. I had to act now, and if by impulse, I pulled my winds to myself, letting them brew and grow in strength. At least I could distract the sand devil while Ulika escaped.

Except, as I gathered my magic, the creature split until it was no longer one but three sand devils, growing in strength as they roared toward me. I had just enough time to toss words over my shoulder. "Ulika, run!"

A gust blew around me, hard, and I lost my footing, but it did not matter. My magic lifted me above the ground and hurled me into the midst of the sand devils. Chaos roared around me, and whiteness invaded my vision. I was weightless, breathless, and slowly my strength ebbed away, as though I was tethered to something that sucked away my energy.

Faint screams came from beyond the storm, and a wave of heat surged around me. The blast hurled me out of the whirlwind and tossed me against the wall. I landed with a jarring thud but quickly got to my feet. The three sand devils came to a standstill, somehow diminished in size. They smoked from the blast, and their skin had turned to white ash, crumbling off their arms and legs as they approached. A flame smoked on the ground, and I turned to see where it had come from.

Ulika stood at the end of the steps, one hand outstretched, and a light glowed on her palm. A light that should not have been possible. I glanced from her back to the sand devils. She had done this, and yet she had no magic. How had fire come from her? I snuck a glance up at the opening to see if perhaps another god had come down to trick us, but from all appearances, we were alone.

Ulika took another step, and her wide-eyed, panicked gaze met mine. With the blood smeared across her face, a surge of protectiveness rose deep inside me. I lunged toward the sand devils, and they growled, torn between racing toward me or Ulika. She sprinted toward the lamp, grimacing as she put weight on one leg. The three sand devils shifted, their ashy skin slowly merging as they turned back into one monster instead of three.

Lowering its horns like a bull, it dashed toward Ulika.

She let out a little shriek as she clutched the lamp, and it tore through my heart. I summoned my magic —at least, what was left of it—cursing as weakness filled me. What did the gods expect from me? Without access to my magic, I'd fail to kill the sand devils, Ulika would die, and...I didn't know what would happen to me. Nor did I particularly care at the moment. I blasted across the small space as Ulika lifted her hands, and suddenly a sucking came, followed by a blinding whiteness. A blow struck my stomach so hard I crumpled to the ground. An intense pain seized my chest like hands were inside me, squeezing my heart, intent on ripping it out.

I cried out, my fist slamming into the ground, and everything stopped. My entire world went silent, like I had been cast back into the lamp, except I still lay on the ground in the chamber. Opening my eyes, I sat up, pressing a hand to my heart to stop the ache there.

My fingers tingled. A stir of magic filled me, then ballooned. I was free. Free from the lamp, with full access to my magic. The curse had been broken, and I was no longer bound to Ulika. A light and fluttery sensation confirmed my winds had returned, with a promise that I could fly away on the evening breeze to wherever my heart desired.

Victory billowed inside, followed by the taste of ash in my mouth. Ulika lay on the ground, and beside her was the lamp, with white smoke drifting out of it. The edges of her dress, besides being torn, were also charred with fire. Smudges covered her palms, and I rushed to her side, refusing to believe she was dead. Her chest rose and fell as I cradled her in my arms. Then she opened her soft brown eyes, a slow smile coming to her lips as her fingertips grazed my cheek. Oh, the feel of her; I wanted to hold her in my arms forever and take her someplace where she'd be safe, happy, far from the whims of the gods.

"Ulika," I breathed, as if saying her name would tell her everything I felt.

Her smile grew brighter but only for a moment, as her eyes clouded over. Dropping her hand, she turned away from me. "It's over. We're free."

I opened my mouth as her meaning sank in. We were free. From each other. Something had changed her mind while I was inside the lamp, and suddenly it didn't matter what had happened, nor where the sand devils had disappeared to. I had to make her understand that I still loved her. I wanted a lifetime with her, and only her.

"Ulika, talk to me. What happened while I was in the lamp?"

She pressed her lips together, then squirmed out of my arms. With a heavy sigh, she pointed to the lamp. "The sand devils are in there now. We should destroy it, or bury it."

I nodded. "I will personally see that no one will ever find it again."

"Good," she said, but her voice sounded hollow, not happy. "While we were fighting, fire came out of me, out of my hands. I don't have magic, shouldn't have magic. What does it mean? Did the gods give me unnatural strength?"

A confirmation of magic. The fire had come from her. "I don't know," I said gently, "but I will help you find the answers you seek."

Ulika still wouldn't look at me. "There's one more thing. The god, Tallen, he's the one who put you in the lamp. He told me…"

Her chest rose and fell as she struggled to find the right words, and that ache in my heart expanded. She'd spoken with Tallen, and I could only guess at the poison he'd fed her. While gods could not lie, they could focus on a truth that gave someone the wrong impression. I could only imagine what he'd said to her about my past. Still, her first words surprised me.

"We can't be together, Vinn. We can never be. It was all a beautiful dream, but in the end, who we are is too much. You're a god. I'm mortal. You have to let me go. If you don't, they'll take away your divinity, your magic. You've seen what happened here, what the gods did to you, to us. If you disobey their wishes, they will punish us."

My throat constricted like I'd swallowed a stone as her words sank in. The gods would take away the essence of who I was, my very being, and she was right. I'd seen what they were capable of. "We'll find a way," I promised, even though no ideas came to mind. "We'll figure out how to make this work."

Silent tears streamed down Ulika's cheeks. "Don't make this harder than it is. They are gods. No matter where we go or what we do, they will find us and destroy us. I can't live always looking over my shoulder. It's best if you go on, forget me, like you did the others."

"What others?" My question came out sharper than I intended.

Ulika flinched. "Tallen said there had been mortals before me, a pattern of them, and this is, was, your last chance to reform. His actions...it was...almost like he wanted to protect you from something."

"From myself," I muttered darkly. "Ulika, you must know, my past is my past. It's you I love, you I want to spend an eternity with, no one else. Everyone before you was just a pale shadow compared to what we have."

Ulika staggered back. "Please don't do this. You're only making it harder."

I was losing her, and I didn't know what to do to change her mind. Although, it wasn't hers that needed changing but the gods'. No words came to my lips, and we stood in a tense silence until a light glowed.

31
ULIKA

The goddess Justice stepped out of the portal, and despite her overpowering power and apparent disdain for mortals, I was relieved to see her. Her presence ended the conversation between Vinn and me. During the three days he'd been trapped in the lamp, I thought I'd calmed my heart and made a choice not to love him anymore. But seeing him standing tall in all his power and glory brought all the feelings crashing back.

Vinn was everything I wanted. He told me stories, made me laugh, was considerate to both me and my family. He fit in well with my tribe, and with him, the sun shone just a little brighter, and the heat of the day and the cool of the night did not matter as long as he was there. But it was not to be.

I'd already decided what to tell my family when I returned. Alone. Vinn had died slaying the sand devils. They would bother us no more. I'd succeeded in my quest, yet a black hole of emptiness expanded with me. For one blissful moment, I'd had everything I wanted, only for it to be snatched away.

Justice's cold voice jarred me out of my thoughts. "It is finished. You have completed the task set before you in an admirably brief amount of time. I commend you on your swiftness."

She did not sound as though she commended us, for her voice still rang with a firm aloofness.

"Vinn, you shall return to Val Ether with me. We have more to discuss. As for you, mortal, you are free to go. I will take the lamp and hide it. Well done. You have found the magic that lay dormant within you and have set the desert free from the scourge of the sand devils. I must warn you, though, keep what happened here to yourself. If others hear about the magic of wind and fire, they will come searching, and there are only so many times the gods will interfere. In the future monsters will arise in the desert, and it is up to you mortals to use your skills to vanquish them. I will not take your memory from you, but let this serve as a warning. Never go to Fae Mountain again."

I kept my gaze on the ground, nodding as she rebuked me.

"At least let me say goodbye," Vinn said.

I lifted my head as Justice opened a portal and flashes of light lit up the dinginess of the chamber. "You've said it," she snapped.

My lips parted as she snatched his arm and yanked him into the portal.

It closed with a snap, and I was alone in that accursed place.

Bending over, I emptied my stomach onto the ground, then wiping my mouth with the back of my hand, hobbled up the stairs and into the sunshine.

Odd how the sun was still shining, as though nothing had happened in the chamber below. In a few hours, the sun would set, and once again I'd be alone in the cold desert. I sat down on a rock and took the opportunity to rip my dress even further to create a bandage for my ankle. Now it ended right above my knees, and Mama would be mortified if I walked around like this.

Weariness made me sag and I assessed what had happened. Justice had confirmed my suspicion that I had fire magic. It roared out of me when Vinn had been in danger, and afterward, what I'd thought was a fever had cooled, leaving my skin normal. All this time, instead of my being sick, fire had been blooming inside me. What would Anat say when I told her? She'd want me to burn everything. A half smile came to my lips at the thought of her, followed by the heartsickening knowledge I could not share the truth of what had happened to the sand devils.

Suddenly I just wanted to be home, where Papa would make flatbreads and crushed beans, Anat would pester me about my journey, and Mama would scold me for my appearance. I wanted to wash by the river, race boats with the boys, and most of all, I wanted a hug.

It was just my luck that Nika hadn't wandered too far. She'd started back home without me, and a series of calling and waving finally persuaded her to stop. It would have been wise to pause and make camp, but I wanted to be as far away from the chamber of devils as possible, and Nika had no qualms about traveling on into the night.

I slumped over her shoulders, sometimes waking, other times in a lucid sleep. The sky was dark-blue velvet, clear of clouds, and the starry sky shone down on me, lights winking to display a silvery path that led home. Whenever I looked up, the North Star glowed brighter than the others, an omen of a brighter future. That was what I would focus on, not the hollowness in my chest, but the knowledge the sand devils were gone and the journey had given me moments with Vinn to treasure.

At sunrise, I snorted awake to find that Nika had stopped walking to nibble on a dry bush. Barren ground with patches of dried grass stretched in all directions. The crack in the ground was gone, which meant we were lost. I groaned and sat up straight, my shoulders and legs aching when I realized Leban's tribe stood in front of me.

I gasped and stared round-eyed. It wasn't his entire tribe but the drummers and himself, looking ashamed. He stood maybe ten paces away as though he'd been watching me for a while, waiting for me to wake up. I rubbed my eyes again and blinked to make sure it wasn't an apparition. After my adventures in the desert, I wasn't sure if I should trust my vision.

Leban cleared his throat. "We came to apologize."

I raised my eyebrows, impressed.

"We had no choice but to give you over to the goat man. He threatened to destroy our families."

Now that was a threat I understood deeply. How could I hold their actions against them when I would have done the same?

"What he did to you wasn't right though, and he did not warn us against following you. We came to make what we did right, especially because you and Vinn helped us. Without water, our tribe would not survive, and now our source is pure again, thanks to you. As for us, we will do our best to help you."

I straightened my shoulders. This was my opportunity to build an alliance between my tribe and a desert tribe. I choose my next words carefully. "I will forget what happened here if you will assist me on my journey home. Vinn is gone for now." I paused, a lump swelling in my throat. Would he return? Or would the gods send someone else to guard the desert? "I'm going to my people, who dwell by the river, and I would encourage some of you to come with me that we might form a trade alliance."

"It would be agreeable to us." Leban nodded, and his tribe fell into step with Nika.

The journey back to their campsite was much faster, and now that I was surrounded by people again, the nights and days were less lonely. When we arrived at their camp, the tribe welcomed me the way I assumed they'd meant to before Tallen had interfered. I was given a tent, food, water, clothes, and a private place to bathe. Clean and dressed, with a full belly and fresh bandages on my ankle, outwardly I appeared much better, but deep inside, the root of sorrow had taken place. Despite the work I would throw myself into, that it would be a long time before I was happy again.

32
VINN

"You spied on me," I fumed.

Justice and I were back in the halls of Val Ether. Sunlight streamed in, making the walls appear gold, and around me, a crowd of spirits whispered. How much did they care about the world and the lives of mortals? Or where they more concerned with the drama of being amused?

They were relegated to watching instead of participating in life, and it made them lack empathy. Especially for me. I'd, once again, gone against their wishes, and now, thanks to Tallen, the time I'd spent with Ulika and her tribe before the sand devils were freed, was no longer my secret.

"Tread carefully," Justice said, but her attention was focused on the lamp.

I crossed my arms over my chest, fighting down the urge to glare at her. "Did you send Tallen?"

At last, Justice lifted her head. "That's why you are here." Then she turned to the hall and waved her hands. "Tallen, come forth."

His hooves clopped over the stones as he strutted into the golden light, holding his ax in one fist. Thick black brows lowered as he glared at me, as though everything that had happened was my fault. Tallen, I suspected, was jealous of me, and did everything in his power to ruin my peace. He'd also dwelled among the fae for a time instead of with the gods, but he was disliked for his sulky demeanor and actions, driven by envy and spite. Eventually, the gods brought him to the halls of Val Ether—which was what he wanted—to watch over it and prevent those without magic from entering. I hadn't considered that he might want more power and authority, like Justice, and the little he had dominion over was not enough. Which was why he'd interfered with my quest.

A throne sat on a dais, and Justice took her seat under the rays of light. Tallen stood beside me but far enough away that we would not touch, even if we spread our arms. Meanwhile, the spirits gathered, watching the proceedings. My jaw went tight. I didn't like this, didn't want it. Instead, I longed to be free to roam the desert, to show Ulika the beauty of the land, and live, with no one keeping watch and holding me back from my desires.

If this was what it meant to be a god, was it worth it?

"We have gathered to discuss the fate of Vinn, the god of wind, and Tallen, the god of might," Justice began.

She told the spirits of my faults. How, long ago, I'd visited the mortals in their form and pretended to be one of them. She explained how I'd freed the sand devils and caused chaos in the desert, how a mortal had trapped me in a lamp, and with her help and the power of a fire, we'd freed the desert of the blight of those devils.

Next she spoke of Tallen and the task they had given him to guard the halls of Val Ether. She told of his desire to earn a higher place among the gods by meddling in the affairs of others and setting himself up as judge and jury.

"Here I give you two gods who have gone against our wishes. It is unfair to let them walk free without punishment, and so I ask you to decide. Has Vinn, the god of wind, paid for his deeds by freeing the sand devils? Does Tallen, the god of might, deserve punishment for acting against another god without our blessing?"

The last time I'd stood in front of the jury of spirits, they'd sent me to the desert. This time, I wanted to ask for something more, the ability to keep my magic and yet live life with Ulika. But it was impolite to speak out of turn in the hall of the gods, and they would only hold my impudence as another mark against me.

When the spirits ceased their mutterings, Justice rose. "It has been decided. Vinn, you will return to the desert, and if we hear more of meddling with mortals, you shall lose your divinity. You are a god, above such mortal urges, and you shall act in accordance. Tallen, for your misdeeds, you shall go to the far north and defend the highest mountain peaks from the wildest beasts. Once you have learned humility, you may return to our halls."

Tallen growled, a low rumble, but I readied my winds for my return.

33
ULIKA

After an evening of food and drink, and meeting the delightful people of Leban's tribe, I collapsed in my tent, fully intending to fall into a deep sleep. Instead, a light breeze blew, bringing the faint perfume of flowers. There in the dark, my eyes opened, and my heart skipped a beat as I thought of Vinn. Where was he now? We hadn't had a chance to say a proper good-bye, but that was probably for the best. I nestled my head in my arms and closed my eyelids, determined to get some sleep, when the tent flap rustled and a presence joined me inside.

I bolted upright, reaching for my slingshot.

"Ulika, it's me."

"Vinn? What are you doing here?" I asked, breathless.

In response, he swept me into his arms. His thumb brushed over my lips, and his voice was deep and husky with emotion. "I made a promise to show you the world, and I'm going to keep that promise."

My body melted into his despite the words of protest that rose on my lips. "What about the gods? What will they do?"

"Damn the gods. I want you." Vinn snorted and whirled me away.

Resting my face in the crook of his neck, I breathed in his scent and held tightly while we flew. Sweet whispering of wind surrounded us and Vinn's heart thumped in my ear, leaving a thrill of anticipation.

"Open your eyes." Vinn whispered, gently turning me in his arms.

I clung to him as he pressed my back against his chest and held me upright. Slowly I cracked open my eyes, staring down. We were in the starry sky, and below us, clouds drifted lazily, and fire creatures winked, creating dots of light that lit up the blackness. We stood in a sea of stars, both below and above us. Awe and wonder stole my breath away and I held out my palms, letting the fire creatures land on my skin before buzzing away.

"What is this place?" I gasped.

"We're in the gardens of the west," Vinn explained. "Where the lands are verdant and the gardens are beautiful. I've wanted to show you them for a long time. Here's where I find rare spices and herbs, and I want to show you the roots you can dye to create bright colors for your paintings. It's too dark, but when dawn comes, I'll show you everything. There's a cave I've taken shelter in to watch the rainstorms. They are beautiful and dangerous; pellets of ice fall out of the the sky and flatten everything, and the sky roars as though the gods are furious. And when you've seen what's here, there's more, so much more, to show you. The craggy mountain heights, the deep blue sea, the volcanos off the southern coast, and forests thick with trees as far as the eye can see. I'll show you the wild jungles and steaming pools, and cascading waterfalls."

Yearning and gratitude collided as I pivoted to face Vinn. We landed on solid ground and the fire creatures danced around us, giving me a glimpse of his face. I sucked in a deep breath, desire growing as his lips curled into a smile. Lips I very much wanted pressed against mine. His fingers moved up my back, drawing my hips against his as he claimed my mouth with his. He tasted like hope and even though a warning about the gods poked into my mind, I banished the thought and focused solely on him, and the delightful sensations his touch created.

After a long, delicious moment, he broke the kiss, lips brushing mine as he spoke. "Ulika, I want you to hear this from me. When I married you in front of your tribe, I meant it. I love you, not because you are young and beautiful, but because of your heart. Your presence fills all the hollow places in my soul, and the way you care about the lives of others more than you care about yourself is admirable. You insist on putting the needs of others first and yourself last, but you deserve so much more. It would be an honor to live a lifetime with you, even if it means giving up divinity. I went to the hall of the gods, and all they did was pass judgment on one another. There is no joy, no celebration, only a battle for worthiness, and I do not want that to be my legacy. Even if they find us and punish us, your love will be worth it."

“Vinn,” I gasped, a tear sliding down my cheek. “Every word you say is beautiful, and if only it were possible. You don’t understand the guilt I’d feel if the gods took away your magic, your divinity. I’ve loved you for so long, especially when I assumed you were mortal, and it makes me heartsick to know that this cannot be. The years of your life are everlasting, and one day, you might resent me for the future you lost.”

“That’s not possible.” Vinn wiped away my tear with his thumb. “Don’t you understand that a life with you isn’t a loss, it’s a gain? We can travel and have children, and your tribe will be blessed.”

Doubts still rose in my mind, but I let him kiss me, wishing time would stand still, just for tonight and tomorrow while we basked in the gardens.

But a dry female voice jolted us apart.

“I see you did not heed the words of the gods,” said Justice.

She strode out of starlight, and a strange glow hovered about her as she frowned at us. “Vinn, the gods were clear when they said you should stay away from the mortals, yet here you are, flagrantly disobeying."

Vinn held me tight, his hand protectively around my waist. "Leave her alone," he ordered roughly.

Justice waved a hand and huffed. "I did not come to harm you but to explain what happens next."

I stiffened, my cheek pressed against Vinn's chest. I willed myself to breathe as I threaded one of my fingers through his. *Please, don't let the gods take him away and leave me stranded in the gardens. Please let us be.*

And then the words burst out of my mouth. "Just give us one night and one day together before you rip us away, please."

34
VINN

The longing and hope and pain in Ulika's voice almost broke me. It was the same as when she'd come to Fae Mountain, begging for help against the sand devils, at her wit's end, to save her people and sacrifice herself. Again, it was her selflessness, her heart, that drew me to her, how willing she was to protect me, to ensure nothing was taken away that would drive us to resent each other.

"I have watched both of you," Justice went on. "And I wondered if your love would be pure and true. Whether you would succumb to the will of the gods or forget all and act of your own accord. It is clear that no matter what we say or do, you shall not be kept apart. As a result, Vinn, you shall be the god of wind no more, nor welcome in the hall of the gods. Instead, you will be the king of wind, known as a jinn. If any asks where you come from, you will explain you come from the fae, those are your people now, not the gods. You will retain your wind magic and the ability to teleport across the world as you do now.

"As for you, Ulika, you are a fire mage, and shall keep the magic of fire. You also have the ability to teleport across the known land using the power of fire. But be warned, with each blessing comes a curse. Your family line will be tied to the fate of the lamp, and if your offspring are not careful, they might become trapped in it. When that happens, they will be forced to grant three wishes, and may not escape their fate unless someone wishes them free. Keep watch for those who seek to entrap your magic, and do not come to the hall of the gods again. You have chosen your path, and a day will come when your long life will end and you will die. Such is the way of mortality."

Relief sagged through me. This—this was no punishment but a breath of fresh air for a dying soul, a rebirth.

“Thank you, thank you, Justice, for giving us a chance,” Ulika gushed.

“It is both a blessing and a curse,” Justice said. “Use your time wisely, and guard your magic well. There may come a day when the lamp will change the course of magic in all the land.”

Justice turned to enter her portal and whisk herself back to Val Ether, but I didn’t see her leave. A bubble of joy rushed through me so intense I spun Ulika in my arms while she shrieked with joy. And then we were kissing and crying and laughing all at the same time. For the very first time in my life, I was not only free, but also whole. Complete.

Breathless we lay in the grass, without the watching eyes of the gods and I cradled Ulika in my arms, wondering if I’d be able to ever let go of her.

“Vinn?” Ulika asked, straddling me. “How do you feel?”

“Feel? Alive. More than alive,” I gasped, drawing down her head and kissing her. The weight of her felt good and my fingers curled around the edges of her dress, inching it up.

Ulika squirmed, hands flat on my bare chest, drifting lower to my trousers. "I mean, about not being a god?"

I shifted, almost unable to respond as my need for her intensified. "A god? No. I don't mind at all, but I'm still the king of wind and now you're my queen of fire. But I don't want to think about that right now."

I tugged her dress over her head. "I want to make love to my wife."

Ulika pressed her hand against my cheek, her eyes liquid as she leaned down to steal a kiss. "Well then, my king, shall we begin?"

35
ULIKA

We spent a night and a day in the gardens, a fevered blur of lovemaking. Occasionally we'd take a break to walk the gardens, picking flowers, gathering herbs and curious plants. I wore roses in my hair, and at times, I pinched myself to see if the gift of the gods was only a dream. But Vinn was always there, and what we had was real, finally without fear of being torn apart by fate.

At last, we decided to have mercy on our traveling companions and returned to Leban's tribe, who wondered what sorcery had whisked me away. They followed us back to the river, where I had the great honor of telling my tribe the story of how the sand devils had been vanquished, only leaving out a few minor details. We feasted and celebrated with our new friends and, the next day, found gold in the river and silver in the caves. It was clear the gods had looked down upon us and decided to bless one who was no longer one of their own.

As the years ticked away, Vinn and I traveled. We established trade routes with tribes, visited the coasts, the mountains, the jungles, the gardens, and the forests. But I preferred the desert, especially on the day I held my firstborn son, Horus. It was only then a dark inkling returned; so far my tribe had been blessed by magic, but the curse of the lamp still blighted the future.

Sunrise became my favorite time of day, when the golden hues cast rich colors over the sand dunes, highlighting the cacti in vibrant shades of green and making the sand glitter. Treasure surrounded us, the waters shimmered, the fish were abundant, and the palm trees bowed under the breeze, brought by the king of wind. Each morning was the start of a new day full of adventure and hope, a gift by which to enjoy life surrounded by family, friends, and most importantly, the man I loved.

ALSO BY ANGELA J. FORD

Join my email list for updates, previews, giveaways, and new release notifications. Join now: www.angelajford.com/signup

Chronicles of the Four Worlds (epic fantasy)

A complete six-book epic fantasy series spanning two hundred years, featuring an epic battle between mortals and immortals.

Legend of the Nameless One Series (epic fantasy)

A complete five-book epic fantasy adventure series featuring an enchantress, a wizard, and a sarcastic dragon.

Night of the Dark Fae Trilogy (romantic epic fantasy)

A complete epic fantasy trilogy featuring a strong heroine, dark fae, orcs, goblins, dragons, antiheroes, magic, and romance.

Tales of the Enchanted Wildwood (fairy tale romance)

Adult fairy tales blending fantasy action-adventure with steamy romance. Each short story can be read as a stand-alone and features a different couple.

Tower Knights (fantasy romance)

Gothic-inspired adult steamy fantasy romance. Each novel can be read as a stand-alone and features a different couple.

Gods & Goddesses of Labraid (epic fantasy)

A complete epic fantasy duology featuring a warrior princess with a dire future who embarks on a perilous quest to regain her fallen kingdom.

Lore of Nomadia Trilogy (epic fantasy romance)

The story of an alluring nymph, a curious librarian, a renowned hunter, and a mad sorceress as they seek to save—or destroy—the empire of Nomadia.

One Winter Night (fantasy romance)

Winter-themed spicy fantasy romance. Each novel is a stand-alone and features a difference couple.

Visit angelajford.com for autographed books, exclusive book swag and book boxes.

ABOUT THE AUTHOR

Angela J. Ford is a bestselling author who writes epic fantasy and steamy fantasy romance with vivid worlds, gray characters and endings you just can't guess. She has written and published over 30 books.

Aside from writing she and her husband own a marketing agency and provides websites, book fulfillment and marketing services for authors.

She also runs The Signed Book Shop. A one-stop shop for readers to find signed books and book merchandise.

If you happen to be in Nashville, you'll most likely find her enjoying a white chocolate mocha and daydreaming about her next book.

facebook.com/angelajfordauthor
instagram.com/angelajfordbooks
amazon.com/Angela-J-Ford/e/B0052U9PZO
bookbub.com/authors/angela-j-ford
tiktok.com/@angelajfordauthor

www.ingramcontent.com/pod-product-compliance
Lightning Source LLC
Chambersburg PA
CBHW070538310726
48982CB00010B/1401/J

* 9 7 9 8 9 8 5 8 4 8 8 0 9 *